I still had fait... ...re the day was ... ...nt into the famil... ...ice some magic tricks on my brother. Every time I finished a trick I'd glance at the telephone.

But no Perry.

After dinner I resigned myself to taking the plunge. I went to my room, closed the door, and with nervous fingers put through the call. On the fourth ring a woman answered.

"Hello, uh, um, is Perry there?" I managed to say.

"No," the woman responded. There was a long pause, and then she added, "Perry's over at Lana's, but he should be back in about an hour. Would you like to leave a message?"

"No, no message," I said. I hung up quickly.

For the longest time I sat on my bed, the phone in my lap, staring at the wall opposite me as if I were in a trance. But the reality was all too real to ignore. There could be only one reason why Perry would be spending the evening with Lana.

Magic Moments

Debra Spector

BANTAM BOOKS
TORONTO · NEW YORK · LONDON · SYDNEY

RL 6, IL age 11 and up

MAGIC MOMENTS
A Bantam Book / January 1984
Reprinted 1985

ISBN 0-553-17075-9

Published simultaneously in the United States and Canada

Bantam Books are published by Bantam Books, Inc. Its trademark,
consisting of the words "Bantam Books" and the portrayal of a
rooster, is registered in U.S. Patent and Trademark Office and in
other countries. Marca Registrada. Bantam Books, Inc., 666 Fifth
Avenue, New York, New York 10103.

Printed and bound in Great Britain by Hunt Barnard Printing Ltd.

O   0 9 8 7 6 5 4 3 2 1

*For Rob and his invaluable assistance,
and for Straw
and the magic moments we have shared*

Chapter One

Misdirection: the ability to do one thing while others believe you are doing something else. Any magician will tell you that that's the key to every successful illusion ever performed. Even I know that, and I've been doing card tricks for only a year and a half.

But it never occurred to me that misdirection is something that happens in real life, too.

But, I'm getting ahead of myself. I guess I should start with the night it all began, the night of my friend Sara Carter's Valentine's Day party. That was the night I made my formal debut as Nicki Petersen the Peerless, card-handler extraordinaire.

And, not coincidentally, it was the night I discovered how even the best magicians can be fooled. . . .

1

* * *

I was into my routine, having performed half a dozen card tricks for the fifteen or so people gathered around the bridge table set up in Sara's den.

"Pick a card, any card," I challenged, holding out the shiny deck to Sara.

Skeptical, she slipped a neatly manicured finger into the middle of the pack, pulled out a card, and held it up for the rest of the crowd to see.

"OK, now put it back," I told her.

Sara did, and then I shuffled the deck a few times and looked out at the faces staring back at me. I'd already been able to confuse this small audience with my other card tricks, but everyone still looked doubtful. I smiled, pleased by their lack of faith and the apparent interest in what I was going to do next. I couldn't wait to see all my friends' faces when I'd finished the trick.

Shuffle completed, I handed the deck to Sara. "Count out ten cards then turn the eleventh one up." After Sara complied, turning over a six of hearts, I said, "That's your card, isn't it?"

"How'd you do that?" Sara asked, amazed.

"Just lucky, I guess," I said, smiling nonchalantly. Little did anyone know I'd blown this one only that morning, when practicing it for the fiftieth time on my little brother Chris.

"I'm impressed," said Sara's on-again, off-again boyfriend Carl.

"Me, too," said Angie, a friend of mine from school, echoing the feelings of the rest of the crowd. "Do another."

"If you insist," I said offhandedly, as though I didn't care whether they were interested in my performance or not. Actually, I loved doing card tricks, and I was thrilled to see people enjoying my performance.

Yet as much as I enjoyed the opportunity to show my stuff, putting on the show that night hadn't been my idea. Sara had talked me into it, insisting that her party would be a bust without some entertainment. Never having performed for a real audience before, I was a little unsure. I knew that performing this way would be a far cry from informally taking out a deck of cards in the school cafeteria in front of my closest friends, and I was a little scared of failing. But I was willing to try, and now I was glad I had. Everybody seemed to be enjoying my routine, and it felt good to be liked and appreciated. Anyway, I suppose I was a welcome change from a rock band—not to mention considerably cheaper.

After I reshuffled the deck, I called out, "Anyone here into extrasensory perception?"

A few heads nodded. "Well, you're all in for a treat," I told them. "I'm going to pick another card, but this time I'm going to use a little ESP to help me along. And just to prove that these aren't trick cards or anything, I'm not even going to touch the deck. Carl, you want to help me on this?"

"Sure," he said a little reluctantly.

"You've never seen the trick before, have you, Carl?"

"No."

"That's for those of you who think I've planted a stooge," I said. Actually, shy Carl would have been the last person I would have picked to assist me, but I was doing it as a favor to Sara, who was trying everything she could—including throwing this party—to get him interested in her again.

Why she was going to all this trouble, I wasn't sure. Carl certainly was good-looking, with strong, broad shoulders and curly blond hair, but in my opinion looks were all he had going for him. I thought Carl was boring, and I couldn't really understand why Sara wanted him to be her boyfriend.

"OK, Carl. I'm going to turn my back, and when I do I want you to count out any number of cards between ten and twenty. Stop any time you like and show that card to the rest

4

of the group. Then put all the cards back on the deck."

After Carl had followed my instructions, he said, "I'm ready. Now what?"

"You just stand there and smile while I turn around and shuffle the cards." Taking the deck from Carl's outstretched hand, I carefully halved it and did a quick jog shuffle. Then I counted out twenty cards, and pointing to the twenty-first on top of the deck, I told Carl to turn it over. "Is that your card?" I asked, already knowing the answer.

"Amazing" was Carl's only response.

"Let's see that again," another girl said.

Just then Sara eased herself through the crowd. "I think it's time we gave Nicki a break," she said. "Besides, the pizzas are ready. I don't know about any of you, but I'm starved."

While everyone else began to drift slowly toward the serving table in the dining room, I folded up the green felt cloth I'd spread out on the card table. I was just about to stuff the cloth into my bag when I happened to look up. There was a dark-haired boy standing nearby. I hadn't noticed him during my performance, and he didn't look like anyone I'd seen around school. He wasn't too tall—maybe five-eight or so—and from the shape of his slim body and narrow waist, he looked like he could be a runner. Then I noticed his eyes—dark, shiny pools that were examining me curiously, as if I were a lab specimen under a microscope. He made me feel a bit self-conscious.

"Something on your mind?" I asked straightforwardly. I didn't want to let him know how uncomfortable I felt.

"What makes you say that?" he asked, sounding a little startled by my abrupt question.

"Well, are you always in the habit of staring at a person like you have X-ray vision?"

"Was I doing that?" he asked as he slowly approached the card table. He sounded genuinely surprised.

"Don't you keep track of what your own eyes are up to?" I asked, but he didn't answer. I continued to do a little examining of my own, and at second glance, his eyes weren't as cold as I'd imagined. They were just . . . inquisitive. And while his face would never win any beauty contests, it was definitely intriguing. It was slightly rugged, with a nose that seemed to bend a little to the right, and a neat, chiseled jawline; in short, it was a face with a lot of character. I hadn't come across many boys with character since moving to Southern California seven months earlier.

"Where did you learn to shuffle like that?" he asked almost slyly.

The question surprised me. "What difference does it make to you?" I shot back defensively. The inflection in his voice didn't tell me whether he meant it as a criticism or a compliment, and I had always had a hard time with criticism.

"Do you always answer a question with another question?"

"Do you?"

The boy's eyes softened. "I didn't mean to pry. I was just surprised. I've never seen a girl shuffle cards like that before."

"What you meant to say was, 'You shuffle like a guy.'" It was funny, I thought. He didn't look like a male chauvinist type. But if all he wanted to do was bug me for being a girl magician, I wanted no more of this conversation, interesting face or not. I was still holding the green felt, and now I bent down and shoved it into my carryall.

"I wasn't knocking you," he said apologetically. "I—I was trying to compliment you. It's not too often you see a girl doing card effects. I was just wondering where you got into close-up magic, that's all."

I looked up from my bag. The boy's lips had turned up into a shy smile that I couldn't help being affected by. I must have been reading him wrong at first—not, by the way, the first time I'd done that with a boy. I was shy myself about meeting new guys, and sometimes I got defensive to cover up my fear. Dropping the bag onto the floor once again, I gazed into those dark, shiny eyes.

"I guess I was a little hard on you. Sorry," I said, trying to make amends. "I picked up the shuffle from a boy I knew in Michigan; the card tricks came later, all from books. End of story."

"Or maybe the beginning," he said. "You're pretty good. Have you ever thought about performing for real?"

"Well, I performed for real tonight—just now."

"This *was* a great performance," he said, his dark, almost black, hair reflecting the overhead light as he shook his head. "But I'm talking about performing for people who aren't your friends. You know, professionally."

I couldn't tell if he was kidding. "You think I'm really that good?" I asked.

"Could be. To tell you the truth, my cousin dragged me here on the pretext that a real magician would be on hand. So far, I haven't been disappointed."

"Thank you," I said. I was beginning to like this guy more and more. "Are you a big magic fan?"

"You could say that," he answered simply.

"Have you ever seen the Super Cut?" I asked excitedly.

Before the boy had a chance to answer, I pulled a deck of cards from my bag and began to shuffle them in my hands. "Pick one," I said confidently.

Looking slightly amused, the boy extended his long, slender fingers into the outspread deck and selected a card.

Suddenly I began to feel nervous. The boy's all-knowing expression puzzled me, and I wondered if maybe he was just humoring me. With my luck he'd probably invented the trick. "Now put the card back in the deck, anywhere at all," I said, feeling my confidence slipping.

The boy placed the card in the middle of the deck. I proceeded to shuffle then count out the cards into four piles of thirteen. Turning over the top card on the first pile, I said, "This is your card."

The boy shook his head, and to my amazement he looked worse than I felt. "I don't know what went wrong," I said, feeling flustered and more than slightly embarrassed. "It worked when I did it for my brother this morning."

"Would you like to see where you made your mistake?" Without another word he took the cards from the table and squared them. After a quick shuffle he offered me the deck again. "Pick one," he said, his face expressionless.

Maybe I should have been upset by the way this guy was showing me up, but I honestly got the impression he really wanted nothing more than to correct me. I liked that, especially since

I was really baffled. Following his instructions, I chose the four of clubs and quickly put it back near the right edge of the deck.

Repeating my earlier moves, the boy counted out the cards on the table. "Here's where you went wrong," he said, using the same professorial tone of voice Mr. Metzger uses when correcting my computer math problems. "The card will always be on top of the *second* pile." He picked up the cards and handed them to me.

"Of course," I said, understanding my mistake. "I should have known that."

"Don't let it bother you," he answered, his voice turning softer. "That effect is very sophisticated. I'm impressed you even attempted it."

"I like a good challenge," I said. "I can see that you do, too. How long have you been doing card tricks?"

"Oh, I don't do them," he said.

"Well, what you just did sure looked like one."

"What I mean is, that effect happens to be one of the few I know. My grandfather taught me. In fact, he gave me a book by Dai Vernon that's got some unbelievable things in it. It's incredible what can be done with a simple deck of cards."

"Hmm, I'm not familiar with the book," I said. I wasn't even sure who Dai Vernon was, though I assumed he was a magician of some sort.

"You really ought to check it out," he said. "You could borrow it from me if you want. I could also probably show you some of the more involved stuff myself. You can't always get a clear picture from books."

"I could use some lessons," I admitted. I found the boy's willingness to help me very appealing.

"Hey, do you know how to do a Tenkai palm?"

"No."

"That's another thing Pops showed me. Let me have a card." I gave him the top card on the deck, a three of spades. At least I think I gave it to him. I was sure I'd placed it in his left hand, but the next thing I knew it was gone.

"How'd you do that?"

"It's an old magician's effect, but you look like you can keep a secret." He put the card back in his palm and repeated his moves in slow motion. This time I could see how he deftly flipped the card from his palm to his wrist and up his sleeve. "Now it's your turn," he said, handing me the card.

I'd already mastered a basic palming technique, so I thought there would be nothing to it. But every time I tried to move the card to my wrist, it fell to the floor. I was determined to get it right, though, and I guess that must have been obvious by my strained expression.

"I think that's enough for now," he said, smiling, gently taking the card from me after what must have been my fifteenth attempt. "It took me months to get that one down. Just keep practicing, and if you get it right, maybe one day I'll show you some of Pops's other maneuvers."

My heart always has this nasty habit of going into overdrive whenever I'm attracted to someone, and, sure enough, it was beating rapidly now. I was especially excited by his apparent desire to see me again. From the way his intense eyes bored into mine, I couldn't help imagining this boy just might have something more personal in mind than showing me card tricks. I hoped that wasn't just wishful thinking on my part.

"That would be great," I said.

"I'd read up on Vernon's techniques, too, if I were you. It couldn't hurt."

"I can use all the help I can get—especially from someone like you who seems to know what he's doing. Maybe we could get together sometime soon, like during the next few weeks or something."

I realized that I must have said something wrong because the boy looked down at his feet, his smile gone. He seemed very uncomfortable, and pretty soon I began to feel uncomfortable, too, and a great silence fell between us. I knew I should say something, just to get us started talking again, but I couldn't. I wasn't used to being the aggressor when it came to boys. In fact, I was shocked at how aggressive I'd already been with this guy.

We might have stood there like two statues separated by our thoughts for the rest of the night, but the silent pause between us was suddenly shattered by Sara's voice from the kitchen. "Last call for pizza. It's going fast."

"I—I guess the pizza isn't going to wait around too much longer," I said, relieved to have something to say. "Would you like a slice?"

"Pizza," he repeated, as if it were a foreign word. "That would be good."

"Stay here. I'll be right back," I said, backing into the dining room.

Whistling to myself, I turned in the direction of the food but was stopped by Nick De-Grande. *Oh, no, not now,* I said to myself. Nick was an all-right guy—in fact we were good friends—but ever since the first day I'd sat next to him in American history, he'd gotten it into his head that the two of us were destined to be a couple. ("Nick and Nicki—it's a natural," he was always telling me.) I couldn't see it happening, though. Nick *was* fun to talk to and to be around, but the thought of kissing him always made me feel sick.

Now Nick swung his skinny arm across my shoulder. "Uh, Lisanne and I really thought you were good tonight, Nicki," he said.

Lisanne? Approaching us from the kitchen was Lisanne George, a cute-looking brunette who'd had her eye on Nick for a long time. I hadn't noticed them together before. Hmm, maybe the two of them had finally connected, I thought with relief. "Thanks. That's nice of you to say," I told them.

"But Lisanne and I are having an argument," Nick continued. "She thinks you were using a trick deck, but I know it was the real thing. Could you do a trick for us now and settle it?" Without waiting for an answer, he thrust a deck into my palm, adding, "I got these from Sara."

With one eye on the pizza and my thoughts still in the den, I dutifully shuffled the deck and performed a quick, simple hidden-card trick. Impressed, Nick turned to Lisanne and smiled. "See? Satisfied now?"

"Thanks, Nicki," Lisanne added.

With that out of the way, I hurried to the table, grabbed two paper plates, and looked over the four remaining slices of pizza. One was plain, two had mushrooms and sausages, and the last had everything but the kitchen sink on it. I debated over which one to select for my magical friend. *Wow, I don't even know his name,* I realized, amazed that my usually methodical mind had forgotten to pick up that vital piece of information. Anyway, I decided against the deluxe slice right away, figuring that my magician wouldn't be as thin as he was if he ate pizza like that regularly. He might like the sausage and mushroom—but what if he didn't? I knew I might stand there all night without making a decision, so I finally chose the plain slice and one with sausage and mushrooms. I figured I'd give him first choice, since I'd be happy with either.

Pleased with my decision, I turned and happily headed back to the den. "Here's the p—" I stopped when I realized he was gone. Puzzled, and still holding a plate in each hand, I searched through the crowd, looking for that head of dark hair. *Where are you?* I wailed inwardly after checking the living room, dining room, kitchen, and patio. My trip through the rest of the house revealed nothing but two empty bathrooms, a room filled with jackets and pocketbooks, the closed door to Sara's mother's room, and a couple kissing noisily in Sara's bedroom.

By the time I worked my way back to the den, I was really angry at the nameless magician. Who did he think he was to walk out on me like that? Nobody had ever done anything so cruel and heartless to me before—and I didn't like it one bit.

After a while my anger subsided, replaced by a sort of aching feeling of disappointment. It was a feeling I hadn't experienced since the night I realized I'd never see Gilly again. That confused me even more. How could a few minutes with someone whose name I didn't even know have affected me as strongly as all those months with the boy I'd once promised I'd love forever and ever?

Depressed, I returned to the den and perched on the edge of the brick hearth. There was no doubt about it; this loss was just as real as that other had been back in Michigan. The boy was gone, vanished into thin air.

Well, Nicki, it was fun while it lasted, I tried to console myself. The only thing to do was to go back to the living room and try to enjoy myself. When I got there, I looked around and saw that everyone had fallen into couples, and I realized that if I tried to talk to any of these intimate pairs, I would feel like an intruder. Even Sara was huddled up in a corner with Carl, and had that don't-bother-me-world look on her face.

There was nothing left for me to do but try

to fill the empty feeling inside me the only way I could. I ate both pizza slices quickly, not even minding that they were cold now. Then I went back to the table for the deluxe slice and ate that one, too.

Chapter Two

Sara jogged up to my house early the following morning. "C'mon, sleepyhead," she called through the open screen door. "We're late."

"Since when are we on a schedule?" I said grumpily, walking slowly to the door, my blue Nikes in my hands. It was hard for me to get up early for school, let alone on the weekend, but Sara had long ago shamed me into joining her and Caroline Austin on their early morning jogs. "Besides, it's Sunday, the day's wide open," I felt compelled to add.

"Maybe your day is free, but I've got, er, other plans," Sara hinted mysteriously.

"Do tell," I said, dropping down on the front porch to put on my running shoes.

"Carl's taking me on a picnic at Hansen Dam this afternoon," Sara said gleefully, sitting down next to me on the step. "After this I've got to go back and wash my hair and do my nails and decide what to wear."

"That should take you all morning at least," I said, nudging Sara playfully with my elbow while I tied my laces.

Sara pouted. "That's not funny. Nothing fits me anymore."

"That's terrific," I said. "What have you lost, five, six pounds now?"

"Eight and three-quarters," she said proudly. "Though I may have put back a few ounces with the pizza last night. Maybe I should have served salads."

"And let everyone else suffer along with you? The pizza was great. Believe me, I know. Besides, you can work it all off now."

"Good thinking, Nicki. We'll go all the way up to Devonshire and back today. We can all use the workout, and it'll give us a chance to talk. What d'ya say, pal?"

"Yeah . . . sure," I agreed reluctantly.

I must have been crazy—or still asleep—not to have put up a fuss. I had just committed myself to a good five-mile jog—I, who found the two-block sprint to the mailbox tiring. My matching blue sweat pants and sweat shirt maybe made me look like I was ready to tackle the marathon, but these bones of mine would have given anything to be lying back in bed at that moment.

It was funny, I thought; anyone looking at the two of us would have thought I was the athletic one. I *look* all right, with a nice head of sandy blond hair, brown eyes, and a sort of average body that's got everything in the right proportion, but my body *feels* like it's made out of Jell-O. Now Sara, on the other hand, looks out of shape, but all of her thick bulges are solid muscle. She's broad in the shoulders, too, which makes me believe she'll never have the superskinny body she's always dreaming about.

Sara and I got up and headed next door to pick up Caroline. As usual, she was ready and looked terrific in a designer jogging suit. Caroline has these gorgeous long legs and a great tall body, but you'd never know it from the hunched up way she carries herself. She could probably get any boy she wanted to notice her if only she stood up straight, but all she seems to care about is getting good grades so she can become a doctor.

Since she's my next-door neighbor, Caroline was the first girl I met after moving to Los Angeles. She helped me adjust quickly to life here in the San Fernando Valley and was very generous with her time and her friends. Like Sara, for instance. The two of them had been best friends for years—one of those situations of opposites attracting—but Caroline immediately included me in their friendship, secrets, and activities.

"Caroline, you missed the party of the year," I told her as we started jogging down the sidewalk.

"I couldn't help it," she said. "The team bus got back from Ventura really late, and I was so tired I went straight to bed. So tell me what happened."

"No, you tell me first," I said. Caroline was one of the first-stringers on our school's academic decathlon team, a sort of varsity sport for intellectuals, where each member of the team is asked to answer questions and write essays in several subject areas. Our team competed with teams from other schools and hoped to go to the state championships in the spring.

"We won," she said nonchalantly, as if it were no big deal. Deep down I knew she felt differently.

"Well, you'll be happy to know that our friend here won, too, sort of," I said, looking over at Sara. "She and Carl are going out again."

We rounded the corner of our street and headed north, the bright sunshine bathing our backs with warmth. It was one of those picture-perfect Southern California days, the kind I used to dream about this time of year back in Michigan, where I had to put on three pairs of long johns before I could even consider opening the front door. The only signs of winter here on the West Coast were the snow-capped tops of the San Gabriel Mountains off in the distance. Because it was February and well beyond what is known locally as the smog season, the air was clean and sweet smelling, too.

"Yeah, I was a hit at my own party," Sara told Caroline as she adjusted the sweat band on her forehead. "I knew if I gave him enough time, he'd come around. But I wasn't the only one who scored some points last night, I noticed." She turned and aimed a finger in my direction.

"Me?" I said between breaths. "Yeah, my card tricks went over really well."

"I wasn't talking about that. I mean that guy you were talking to afterward. Who is he?"

I was about to answer, but suddenly both Sara and Caroline quickened their pace, and I had to practically break into a run to keep up with them. "Funny, I was going to ask you the same question," I said a minute later, panting heavily. "After all, it was your party."

"What? Wait, I didn't hear you; say that again."

"Only if you guys slow down."

Sara must have been really curious because she immediately downshifted to a slow trot. Caroline slowed down, too. "He's a mystery boy—there one minute, gone the next. I never even got a chance to ask him his name," I said.

"You're kidding! Don't you know that's the cardinal rule of pickups?" Sara exclaimed. "Too bad. He looked pretty nice."

"Well, easy come, easy go," I said wistfully.

Sara wasn't convinced by my tone. "I'm surprised you'd say that," she said. "I really thought he looked interested in you. In fact, I'm sure of it."

"So why did he leave, Miss Know-It-All?"

"I don't know. Maybe he had an early curfew or something."

"Wait a sec, girls," Caroline interrupted. "Something's not connecting here. Sara, you mean to tell me you threw a party and invited someone you didn't know?"

"I didn't invite him. I never saw him before last night. He must have tagged along with someone I did invite. In fact, I didn't even notice him until I spotted him with Nicki."

I wiped away a few drops of sweat. "Look, these things happen. You strike up a conversation with a guy at a party, he seems interested, but then backs off. He was probably just being polite."

"Why am I getting the impression you don't really believe that?" Sara said.

"Well, I *was* having a good time with him," I admitted, "and I wish I'd gotten to know him

23

better, but I've been around enough to realize I'm not going to be asked out by every guy who tosses a few kind words in my direction."

"This just goes to prove we do it all wrong in America," Caroline said. "You wouldn't have to go through grief like this in other countries, you know, Nicki. Take Portugal, for instance. In some villages over there they set aside one day a year for dating. The first boy a girl spots on that day becomes the one she takes as her mate. No hassle, no fuss—"

"And no choice," I said.

"Nicki, if you could see this guy again, would you want to?" Sara asked.

"Sure," I replied. "You know how picky I am when it comes to guys."

"I'll say. Up to now no one has been as good as Gilly," Caroline said.

"That's right. And if this boy had been like any of the others I've met in the Valley, I'd say forget it. But I'd be curious to find out more about him."

"Didn't he give you any clues?" Sara asked.

"Well, he did say he came to the party with his cousin. And he seemed to know a lot about magic—that's what we talked about mostly."

"That doesn't give me much to go on," Sara said. "But I'll ask around, see what I can find out about this mystery boy for you."

"Would you really?" I could feel my spirits

rise, though truthfully I wasn't sure whether it was Sara's words or the sight of the busy street ahead of me that did it. "Look, there's Devonshire!" I shouted, as if spotting an oasis in a desert.

Sara giggled. "Don't get your hopes up," she warned as we neared the busy street. "We're only halfway there."

"Oh, go run a marathon," I grumbled.

As I unlocked the front door of the house on Tuesday afternoon, I heard the telephone ring. I dropped my books, my bag, and my keys on the floor as I hurried to answer it.

"Hello," I said, breathing heavily into the family-room extension.

"Now that's a switch. Usually you hear the heavy breathing when you answer the phone, not when you dial someone else."

"Hi, Sara. I just got in. And Chris obviously can't be bothered to answer the phone." I cast an angry glance at my thirteen-year-old brother, who was sitting in front of the TV playing a video game.

"I knew it was for you," he said. "Sara's been calling every five minutes."

"Where have you been?" Sara asked. "I've been trying to get you for hours!"

Fortunately the phone had a long cord. I picked it up and walked into the dining room, out of earshot of my snoopy brother. I closed the shuttered doors of the family room behind me. "Today's the day I go down to the reading center, remember?" Every week I volunteered at a local elementary school helping little kids with their reading problems.

"And how are the little devils?"

"Coming along," I said. "It's so sad to see them struggling trying to read—but so satisfying when they can get through a sentence without making a mistake."

"I don't know where you get the patience for that," Sara said. "I think I'd try to read the page for them."

"Look, not everybody's a natural-born brain like you. Learning takes longer for some people. But I'm sure you didn't call for a status report on my problem readers."

"You bet I didn't! I have something you might be interested in. My snooping's paid off. I found out who your mystery boy is."

"You *what*? Who is he?"

"His name is Perry Ingram, and he's Greg Decatur's cousin. He's our age, and he lives someplace down in the Hollywood Hills. He *is* a magician, just as you suspected, and from what Greg told me, he's a pretty good one, too. In fact, he comes from a family of magicians."

"He did say his grandfather taught him some

tricks," I said, pulling on the phone cord. "Does he have a girlfriend?"

"Not that Greg knows of. He doesn't really see too much of Perry. He says Perry spends most of his time hanging out with other magicians at this club he belongs to."

"Hmmm." I sighed. "I wonder where *that* is."

"Don't know. Are you thinking of crashing it or something?"

"No, that would be gross. I just didn't know they had a club for magicians around here. Did Greg say anything about why Perry left all of a sudden?"

"No. In fact he was surprised to hear Perry had been talking to you. I guess Perry never mentioned anything to him."

That settles it, I decided when I got off the phone with Sara. Perry probably didn't mention me to his cousin for the simple reason that I didn't make as strong an impression on him as I'd thought. To me, it had been a magic moment, but it soon would be nothing more than a pleasant memory.

Chapter Three

But getting Perry Ingram out of my mind proved not to be that simple.

I kept telling myself it was Sara's fault that I couldn't forget him, but the truth is that I wouldn't have been dwelling on Perry if I didn't really want to be. Yet it was Sara who continued to bug me about him for the rest of the week. She was so excited at my finding someone I thought I might be interested in that she wouldn't stop talking about him or thinking up ways the two of us could meet again. Of course every time she started in about him I'd try to change the subject. She was making too much of it, I'd tell her; it had been nice to talk to Perry, but there was nothing more to it than that.

But if I really believed my words, why couldn't I stop thinking about him? Late at night, long after my parents and brother were asleep, I'd like awake and fantasize about what a dream date with Perry would be like. For three nights in a row I had the same vision. He'd pick me up in his bright red sports car (of course) and whisk me away to this magical, fantasy world where we'd be entertained by jugglers on unicycles and bears dancing to calliope music and all sorts of magicians who'd make things appear and disappear right before our eyes.

This spectacle would be dazzling, but after a while Perry and I would look across our candlelit table and discover that we had eyes only for each other. We'd get back into his sports car, and he'd drive to the top of Mulholland Drive and park in a secluded spot, and then he'd hold me and hug me and tell me I was the most wonderful girl in Southern California.

Then I'd come to my senses. *All Perry will ever be is a fantasy*, I'd tell myself, as much a fantasy as any I'd created over the years about my favorite rock stars and TV heroes. Or like the fantasies I'd spun more recently about how Gilly would come out from Michigan and hold me in that very special, very real way I'd grown so accustomed to.

No matter what Sara said, I knew I'd never chase after Perry. Although I consider myself pretty confident where clothing styles, school-work, and stuff like that are concerned, when it comes to boys I've never been too confident. I prefer to let boys chase after me.

Having been with Gilly for so long, I'd never really had to develop boy-chasing skills, and since then, I hadn't felt the need to learn. Not knowing how to be aggressive with boys did limit my options, but I also felt safer this way, because if I never went after a boy, I never had to deal with being rejected. Since arriving in California I'd been on enough dates with guys who just didn't do anything for me to realize I'd have to change my ways eventually. But as anyone who's ever tried to change a habit knows, it's a lot easier to talk about it than to do it.

So the odds of my meeting up with Perry again were practically nil. Even so, I was grateful that I'd finally gotten the chance to talk to someone else about magic. Thinking over my debut performance at Sara's party, I came to the conclusion that I'd done all right but that I could improve my act if I learned how to do something more elaborate than the pick-a-card-any-card routines. Suddenly I remembered the book Perry had mentioned during our conversation. Maybe it would have some good tricks in it that wouldn't be too difficult for a novice like me to pick up.

There was only one way to find out.

On Saturday I borrowed my mother's car for the morning and drove down to a store on

Victory Boulevard that had magic tricks, games, masks, and lots of novelty gags that were good to give people as gifts when you didn't know what else to get them. I'd discovered the place not too long after arriving in California, and I'd been amazed at the incredible amount of magic paraphernalia crammed into this tiny store.

When I got there, I found the place deserted, and I eased past the monster masks displayed near the front of the store toward the metal rack near the back that contained books on magic.

"May I help you, ma'am?" came a voice from behind me.

"Ma'am?" I said with surprise. I looked up to see an elderly man with a pinched face coming toward me from the back room. He looked more like a crazy wizard than a magician: he had a fringe of wavy white hair around his bald head, a razor-thin mustache, wire-rimmed glasses, and hunched shoulders. If someone told me he'd been slaving over a caldron in the back of the store, I wouldn't have been surprised.

"Excuse me, miss," he corrected himself. "You looked like a ma'am from where I was. Looks like I need a new pair of specs." The man took off his glasses and cleaned them on the edge of his white frock. "You come in here for something special?"

"I'm looking for Dai Vernon's book on magic."

31

He stroked his chin thoughtfully. "Which one?"

I was stuck. I didn't know he had written more than one. "Uh, the one on card tricks," I said, hoping he had written only one of those.

"You sure you want Vernon? What about this here Harry Lorayne book?" The man removed a paperback from the rack and tried to shove it into my arm.

"No, I already have this one," I lied.

"Well, I can give you this here Garcia," he said, picking up another book. "He's one of the masters, you know."

"I'm looking for Vernon," I said stubbornly.

"I'm out of stock on all of Vernon's works right now," he finally told me. "I could order some for you, if you tell me which ones you want."

"No," I answered quickly. I felt as though something crazy were compelling me. "Do you know anyone who has them now? I really want to get it today."

The old man's lips curled up into an amused smile. "In a hurry are you? Wait right here, I'll go back to the phone and see what I can do."

The man hobbled back in a few minutes, looking very pleased with himself. "You're in luck," he said in a pleasant voice. "There's a store down in Hollywood that can satisfy your wish."

"They've got the book?"

I waited while the man scribbled down the name and address on a note pad. "If they don't have it, nobody will."

"Thanks," I said, taking the slip of paper from his old, wrinkled hand. "I really appreciate it."

"Come back sometime when you're not in such a hurry."

I got back into Mom's Pontiac and headed for the freeway. My mother would have died if she'd known I was driving all the way into Hollywood for a book, but I didn't want to deal with that right now. What could I tell her? That I was looking for a book that would make me a good enough magician to impress a boy I might never see again? It made perfect sense to me in a crazy sort of way, but I knew Mom would think I was wasting my time.

Turning the radio up, I eased onto the Ventura Freeway and let the speedometer inch up toward the speed limit, making sure it didn't go over.

As I neared Hollywood, I slowed down and carefully searched the overhead signs for my exit. I was still pretty unfamiliar with this part of town. I'd been to Hollywood only once, right after we moved, to see a movie at Mann's Chinese Theatre with my parents and little brother. I hadn't bothered paying attention to the route then since all I could think about was how terrible it was to be sixteen and going to the movies with my family. Then again, I couldn't blame my parents; they were as anxious to see the famous sights as any tourist would be.

Anyway, it didn't turn out as bad as I'd expected; I even saw a bunch of other kids my age who seemed to be in the same predicament. I kind of enjoyed trying to put my feet in Marilyn Monroe's and Humphrey Bogart's footprints, although I had made sure no one was watching while I did it. And no matter how seedy the rest of the place looked, I was enchanted with the elaborate Oriental fantasy spires and with the cavernous old movie house.

Here I was seven months later, back in Hollywood, but this time driving by myself and feeling a little bit nervous about it. The freeway exit I wanted came up a lot sooner than I'd expected, and I had to negotiate through three lanes of traffic to get off. A few minutes later I turned onto Hollywood Boulevard, which looked a lot less glamorous in the bright afternoon sun than I'd remembered. Of course the star-shaped brass plaques with celebrities' names etched on them still dotted the sidewalk for blocks; but somehow most of the stores and a lot of the people looked pretty run-down.

After parking the car, I walked along the boulevard in search of the Cinema City Magic

Store. Along the way I passed by the bright purple facade of Frederick's of Hollywood, its storefront mannequins decked out in an array of revealing costumes I'd never have the guts to wear. Maybe Sara and Caroline could come down here with me sometime, and the three of us could have a really good laugh.

As I neared the magic store, a strange thrill of anticipation raced through me. Though it looked small from the outside, the large neon sign overhead made it stand out from the fast-food shops surrounding it. Fittingly enough, Harry Houdini's star was right in front of the place, and feeling like a kid going into a toy store, I walked inside.

The shop was like nothing I'd ever seen before. Its outside appearance was deceptive; beyond the door the store expanded into a wonderland of four aisles that could best be described as a supermarket for magicians. With every step I took, the room seemed to take on a new dimension, an optical illusion that I soon realized was caused by the ever-changing light flickering above.

Down the first aisle I went, passing a collection of masks, false mustaches, and sexy costumes. The entire back of the store was filled with a number of items for big illusion work—boxes for sawing people in half, dove cages, and cages to escape from. I stared at them in awe, trying to figure out how they worked. It was hopeless, and enough to make me turn my attention to the magic equipment in the center aisles of the store.

It didn't take me long to find a Dai Vernon book on card tricks called *Select Secrets.* I picked it up quickly, as if someone else would grab it if I didn't. Then I turned to the glass display counter in front of me and glanced at the assorted collection of trick decks, oversized aces, coins, sponge balls, and other tools for illusionists. In the next section of the display I came across magic wands in more shapes and sizes than I'd thought possible.

I could easily have spent the rest of the day blissfully examining the store's contents. But something stopped me. It was as if one of those magic wands had escaped from behind the counter and waved itself over me. For what I saw next could only have been a product of magic. It was a familiar figure, its reflection mirrored in the display glass to my left. I blinked three times to make sure my eyes weren't playing tricks on me.

They weren't. Standing at the counter next to the big illusions was my mystery boy. Perry.

I stood stock-still, unsure of my next move. What does a girl do when someone she's only fantasized about seeing again actually materializes? *Do I go up to him and comment about the coincidence of seeing each other again?* I thought, panicking. *Or do I slink out of the store, hoping he doesn't notice me?* Suddenly that seemed like the best thing to do. How could I explain my presence here? He would know I was here because of him, I was sure of it; and I couldn't bear that embarrassment.

I knew I was going to have to think of something fast because he began to walk down my aisle. I thought about hiding behind a rack of books and imagined waving a wand to make myself disappear, but it was too late. He spotted me and smiled, looking as surprised as I felt.

I smiled back, glad my reflexes were working the way they were supposed to. *I guess this is where you put all those resolutions about being more assertive with boys into action,* I told myself. Summoning up my courage, I ambled over to him.

"Hi," I said brightly. "Nice to see you again."

"You, too," he said. "Nicki, right? We never did exchange names the other night. I'm Perry Ingram."

"I know," I blurted out.

"You do?"

"Yes, well, Sara told me," I said quickly, blushing.

Perry looked amused. "What brings you all the way down to Hollywood?"

Before I had a chance to think of something clever, he noticed the book in my hand. "Oh, I see," he said, answering his own question. "You really are serious about your cards." He sounded very impressed. "So all that talk the other night wasn't just talk."

"Of course not! I may not be a world-class magician yet, but even Dai Vernon had to start someplace."

He nodded knowingly. "Sometimes the best way to learn is through observation," he said. "Do you get to see many magicians perform?"

"No," I admitted. "I'm pretty new to California, and I haven't known where to look."

Perry hesitated a moment before speaking. "There's a real good close-up man working the House of Cards tonight."

"House of Cards?" I asked.

"It's a magicians' club I belong to, and they have shows all the time."

"I didn't know there was a place like that in L.A."

"There are a few places that feature magicians, but this is the oldest and the best. A lot of world-famous magicians perform there, too."

"Sounds wonderful," I said. "I'll have to go sometime."

"It's for members only—and their guests. . . .

How would you like to see that close-up man tonight?"

"I'd love to," I answered without hesitation. It was beginning to dawn on me that my fantasy might actually have been a premonition of some sort. So far our meeting had been just as I'd imagined it would be.

"Tell you what," he continued, his voice brightening considerably. "Why don't you meet me at the entrance at eight o'clock. Oh, you're in for a real treat. In fact, meet me at seven-thirty, and I'll give you a grand tour of the place. You have a piece of paper? I'll write down the directions for you."

I groped around in my bag, but the only papers I could find were crumpled-up tissues and empty chewing-gum wrappers. Holding out the book, I said, "I'm going to buy this, anyway, so why don't you just write the information down in the front?"

"Sure thing." He smiled, revealing nice even white teeth, except for a slightly chipped one in the front. I was glad to see that. It made Perry more human and, therefore, more real. Naturally, in my fantasy his teeth were perfect.

As Perry began to write, a tall, dark-haired girl with the most gorgeous green eyes I'd ever seen entered the store and walked over to us. "Oh, Perry," she cooed in one of those syrupy voices that boys always seem to fall for. "What's keeping you? You said you'd only be a minute."

"I'm almost ready," he said, smiling at the girl. My heart dropped to my big toe. That was the same smile he'd turned on me just moments before. "Will you wait for me out at the car?"

"OK, fine," she said with a touch of impatience. Before she left, she blew Perry a quick kiss.

I wanted to hide. Who was this girl and why had she blown a kiss to Perry? In my fantasy there were no other girls around, so why did she have to come in and spoil this very real moment?

For his part Perry seemed unaffected by the entire incident and returned to the directions as if nothing had happened. Watching him continue to write, I began to feel a bit less concerned. He didn't really treat the girl like a girlfriend, so maybe she wasn't one. But if that was the case, who could she be? A relative of some sort? Yeah, that was it. She had to be his sister, I concluded in the time it took Perry to finish writing. The dark hair and tawny skin coloring were the same. With that worry out of the way, I was able to return Perry's friendly grin when he handed the book back to me.

"Oh, um, I'm not in the habit of telling girls what to wear, but the club insists on dressy clothes for Saturday night." He looked terribly embarrassed saying that.

"Thanks for the warning," I said. "I'll be there in my finest."

"I've got to go now, Nicki. See you tonight." He waved goodbye as he turned toward the door.

"Wouldn't miss it for anything," I answered.

This is incredible, I thought as I waited in line to pay for the book. I had walked into the Cinema City Magic Store expecting to find a book, and now I was walking out with a date, an honest-to-goodness date. True, I had to drive to the House of Cards myself, which meant that Perry wouldn't be picking me up in his red sports car, but then, not everything in a girl's fantasies can come true.

And I didn't mind settling for what I was getting. Not in the slightest.

Chapter Four

The House of Cards was an old, Spanish-style hacienda high up on a hill in the Pacific Palisades. I could see why Perry wanted me to meet him there—if he had had to pick me up, the round trip to my house and back would have taken him hours. Fortunately, I didn't have any trouble convincing my folks to let me have the car. Both of them were still so concerned that I adjust well to California that they were more than happy to give me the keys. "Just drive carefully," Mom had warned as I left.

Approaching the entrance to the club, I shifted into low and eased up the steep, curving asphalt drive. At the top I was met by a young man dressed in black tie, tails, and top hat. He opened the car door and asked for the keys.

"Uh, what for?" I asked nervously. Visions

of being kidnapped by a mad magician leaped to mind.

"To park the car," he answered wearily.

It was only then I noticed the sign that said Valet Parking. Gulping self-consciously, I handed him the keys and slipped out of the car.

Other cars were continually arriving from which couples in evening wear emerged as I helplessly paced the broad sidewalk at the foot of the steps leading to the club. Perry was right about the dress code here, and I felt a little underdressed even though the powder blue ruffled skirt and blouse I had on was one of my best outfits. At least I was wearing heels, which was no small accomplishment since my feet were shaped like sneakers, not like slim, delicate, tapered shoes. *What if Perry is embarrassed to be seen with me?* I wondered in a panic. Then, peering into the darkness, unable to spot him, I was struck with an even more terrifying thought: *What if he's not here at all?*

I stood out front for a few more minutes and then followed other new arrivals up the twenty or so marble steps to the entrance. I hadn't seen steps like these since my visit to the Michigan state capitol in sixth grade. I hadn't liked the climb then, and I didn't relish it now, either, especially in these heels. My heart pounded in pace with each step upward, and as I climbed I became more and more nervous. The

House of Cards was a private club, and I could get inside only if accompanied by a member. If Perry didn't show, I could look forlorn and hope someone from the crowd would take pity on me and bring me in. Or I could pretend to be a relative of one of the performers and hope the person at the door believed me. Or I could do what Nicki Petersen usually did when faced with a situation like this—turn around and go home.

All the way up the steps, I kept my gaze on my feet, making sure I didn't make a fool of myself and stumble and fall. I guess that's why I didn't see the slender boy with the coal-colored eyes until I was practically on top of him.

"Hi, Nicki. Glad you could make it," Perry said.

I looked up and breathed a huge sigh of relief. "Yeah, those steps can be real killers."

"What?" Perry asked, obviously confused.

I shook my head. "Never mind," I said, grinning. "Glad to see you, too."

Perry took my hand, and I found the unfamiliar touch comforting. "Let's go in," he said. "I think you're going to like this place. As you can imagine," he added, gesturing, "it's pretty awesome."

"I know what you mean. The outside's beautiful," I said. The three-story stone mansion was surrounded by graceful towering palms and thick yucca trees. The cathedral-style picture windows on the first level all seemed to be filled with intricately designed stained-glass figures.

"Just wait till you see what's inside," Perry said proudly, as if about to usher me into his own house.

"This seems to be an out-of-the-way place for a magicians' club," I said.

"Well, it didn't start out as one," Perry replied. "This used to be the home of an old movie star who was a big fan of magicians. When he died, he willed that it be used by the magicians he'd known and sort of kept on as a living memorial to the craft."

Perry stopped his lecture to show his card to the woman at the entrance, but she just waved him through. "Go on, Perry. I see you've got company tonight." She winked knowingly.

"Er, um, yeah," he mumbled, letting me pass by him through the ornately carved wooden doorway.

Once inside, we passed through a narrow, candlelit hall until we came to a tiny room with four closed doors along its walls. "Where are all the people?" I asked Perry.

He smiled mysteriously. "Let's see if you can figure it out."

I tried the handle on the farthest door to my left but pulled back quickly at the sound of a deep, almost mocking laugh. "Oh," I cried out, startled.

"It's all right. That was just to warn you that you were at the wrong door."

"Subtle, isn't he?" I said. "Should I try this one?" I asked, pointing to the door on its right.

Perry just shrugged but looked like he was enjoying my dilemma. Cautiously I approached the door and opened it. Out sprang a wire-mesh net filled with hundreds of playing cards.

"Looks like I toppled the house of cards."

"Everybody's made that mistake at one time or another. Here, try this one," he said, motioning to the next door to the right.

I made a tentative move toward the door. Then, figuring I had nothing to lose, I drew it wide open. I gasped. Inside was a large room, lined on one side with those stained-glass panels I'd seen from the entrance. It was filled with more carved wood panels, a couple of sofas, several sets of tables and chairs, and many of the people I'd seen outside. A small waterfall leading into a fish pond dominated the center of the room.

"Wow" was all I could say.

"This is just the beginning," said Perry.

"Say, what was behind the fourth door?"

"Nothing. It's a fake."

"I should have expected as much from a bunch of magicians."

"Actually I think it was the movie star who put in the doors. He was a bit of a practical joker and built this house as much to amuse his friends as anything. There are tons of hidden rooms and stairways to nowhere in here. Unfortunately, most of them are closed up now."

Perry walked me over to the bar at the far end of the room and ordered sodas for both of us. The bartender, a burly man with a huge, red handlebar mustache, put down the glass he was polishing and winked. "For you, Perry, anything." Then he turned to me and smiled through his whiskers. "Hi, beautiful."

After he placed the frosted mugs in front of us, Perry picked them up and started to leave. "Hey, wait a minute, Perry," the bartender said. "You're not going to run off without introducing me to your pretty girlfriend, are you?"

Sheepishly Perry put the mugs down on the bar. I saw a blush creep into his face. Actually, I also felt a little awkward hearing myself called his girlfriend, although the idea of it was certainly appealing.

Perry motioned for me to sit down, so I perched myself on a leather stool as the bartender leaned over and whispered, "I don't know what's wrong with this guy. He never lets me meet his girls." He extended his hand. "Name's Bert."

"Maybe he's afraid you'll steal them away," I

said, feeling a little distressed to hear him refer to Perry's girls.

Bert twirled his mustache. "Maybe he's right. Let me have your ring."

Puzzled, I looked up from my drink. "Huh?"

"I know you think I'm very forward. But I like you, and people who like each other exchange rings, right?" He pulled a gold and diamond ring from his pinkie. "See? Here's my ring. You give me yours, and I'll give you mine. A token of our friendship."

I thought the guy might have been guzzling too much of the stuff on the wall behind him, but Perry motioned for me to go along with his request. So I handed him the silver ring my dad had given me for Christmas. "Thanks," he said, giving me his own ring. "I'll take good care of it."

From out of nowhere came a gold rope, which he looped through my ring. "As you can see, there's no way the ring can come off this rope. That will insure that I won't lose it, don't you think?"

"Well, yeah, I guess so," I said a bit skeptically. I turned to look at Perry, who seemed to be enjoying this stop on our tour of the club.

In any event, Bert went on talking some nonsense about the joys of owning a ring when all of a sudden he snapped the rope in the air and—*voilà*—the ring was gone.

"Hey, what happened?" I asked.

He shrugged his shoulders. "I don't know. It was here a minute ago, Oh, I'm sorry, beautiful. Maybe it fell into one of these drawers." He pointed to a row of drawers underneath the counter I was leaning on.

"But they're closed." I pulled on one. "And locked."

"I guess I'll just have to get out my keys and open them." From his back pocket, Bert removed a leather-covered key case. Slowly he unzipped it—and inside, on one of the key holders, was my ring! "Oh, silly me. I had it all along," he said.

"That was wonderful," I said with a gasp, thinking that the ring trick would be great at parties. "How'd you do it?"

The bartender frowned and looked at Perry. "Haven't you told her a magician never gives out his secrets?"

"She's a magician, too. A very good one, I might add." He turned to me and smiled warmly before downing the rest of his soda. "We've got to be going now. Ready, Nicki?"

"Wait a sec—I've got to give Bert his ring back," I said as I looked down at the finger I'd slipped it on. "Oh, no—it's gone!"

"Don't worry about it, beautiful," Bert replied, his eyes twinkling. "Looks like this ring has no taste; it likes my finger better than yours.

Look, it must've jumped off your hand and onto mine while we weren't watching."

I looked over at Bert's hand, and there was the ring! I was impressed again and told Bert so.

Then Perry took me out of the big room and down one of several hallways leading to the rest of the building. "That Bert is some character, don't you think?" Perry said.

"Yeah. He's kind of overbearing, but he's also pretty clever. I really would like to know how he got my ring into that case and also how he got his ring off my finger."

"Magic." Perry winked. "Actually, those effects are easier than you think. I'll teach you sometime."

"But what about what Bert said about giving away secrets?"

"That only applies to amateurs. I meant what I said about your being good."

"Thanks," I said, feeling my heart race. "It means a lot to me to hear you say that."

Tentatively he reached out for my hand and grasped it in his. "I'm glad we ran into each other today, Nicki. There aren't many people who truly appreciate magic like you do."

I didn't know how to answer that. In my fantasy this was where we stared at each other over candlelight, but at that moment we were in the middle of a hallway, under a bright crystal chandelier, and surrounded by the Saturday night crowd. It didn't seem like the right place to express my growing feelings.

Actually, the truth was, I was afraid it was too soon for me to tell Perry how I felt about him, so I changed the subject. "Uh, where are we going now?"

A few steps later we reached the entryway to a small room whose walls were lined with shelves filled with magic paraphernalia. At the center of the room was a round table covered with green felt. "Thought you'd be interested in this stuff," Perry said, pointing to the walls. "All those things are antiques." After we looked at the display, he motioned for me to sit at the table and he sat across from me.

"You know, Nicki, all the magic stuff in this room gives off a special aura. It makes the people in the room have the power to see into other people's minds."

I felt that Perry was leading into a trick, but I didn't mind. "How so, Perry?"

"For instance," he said, gazing into my eyes, "the powers tell me that blue is your favorite color."

I smirked. "You don't need magic to figure that out. I *am* wearing blue tonight."

"I get a powerful signal that you feel so strongly about blue that you wear it all the time."

51

"That's true; I do have a lot of blue clothes."
Now how did he know that?

Closing his eyes, Perry raised his arms in the air. "I see more. You have a fondness for children. You work with them . . . You . . . teach them to read."

This was getting weird. "Y-yes," I stammered.

Then he held his fingers to his temples as if he were concentrating deeply. "And I see something else. You have a history exam this week—and you're really nervous about it."

"Hey, how did—? Hey, there's no power in this room," I cried, realizing what he was doing. "I bet Greg told you all that."

Perry grinned sheepishly. "Yeah, but I had you going there for a minute, didn't I?"

Together we laughed at the silliness of his "trick," but I was touched that he'd cared enough to learn more about me, especially since Sara had told me otherwise. My eyes locked with his as I struggled to determine the depth of his interest in me. His dark pupils seemed to soften as we gazed at each other, and as though he had read the feeling in my eyes, Perry reached for my hand across the table. It seemed as though it would be only a matter of seconds before we'd be in each other's arms.

I could hardly believe it. The similarity between my fantasy and what was going on now was so eerie I let out an involuntary gasp.

Perry pulled his hand back. "Is something wrong?"

"Oh, no," I said.

But the mood had been shattered, and Perry made no further attempt to approach me. "Are you sure? You're not upset I asked Greg about you, are you?"

"Not at all. But I'm surprised you mentioned me to him."

"Why?"

"I mean, after the way you left Sara's party all of a sudden."

Perry looked down at the table. "Oh, that. Uh, after you got up, I saw you talking to that guy. You looked like you were busy, so I left."

"But I told you I was only going to get some pizza for us. That guy I was talking to is just a friend from school. Oh, I wish you'd known that."

"You do?" Perry sounded hopeful, but his face betrayed the remorse he felt as he realized how his misunderstanding had made our first encounter end prematurely.

"Sure I do," I said. "I was enjoying our conversation, and then the next thing I knew, you were gone. I was afraid I'd never see you again."

"I have a feeling we would have met again

53

even if you hadn't shown up at the magic store today."

"You mean those tricks you said you'd show me?"

He looked down again as if he were afraid to look me in the eye—or simply embarrassed to express his feelings. I wasn't sure which. "Well, maybe," he said after a moment's hesitation.

"I'm glad it happened this way," I said. "I mean, I wouldn't be seeing this show tonight otherwise," I added quickly so he wouldn't think I was being too aggressive.

"Speaking of the show," Perry said, rising quickly, "if we don't hurry, we're going to be late."

"Where is it?" I asked.

Perry walked me down the hall and into another lounge with a bar. The tension between us was gone now, and Perry was more at ease when he told me, "There are three showrooms. A small theater where close-up magic is done— that's where the magician I told you about will be—and two showrooms for illusionists. We're going to go to one of those first."

Perry led me down another candlelit hallway. This one was carpeted with thick red pile, and the walls were covered with posters advertising performances by Blackstone and Houdini and other famous magicians, past and present.

"Perry, why are we going to see the illusion-ists first?"

"The close-up show doesn't start until much later." Then, to my surprise, he pulled from an inside jacket pocket a pair of long white gloves just like the ones worn by the parking attendant.

"Do they make you put on gloves just to watch the show?"

"No, I just wear them every time I perform," he said casually as he slipped them on.

"You're *performing* tonight?" I cried out. That is, I must have cried it out because a matronly looking woman in front of me turned around to see what the commotion was about. "Why didn't you tell me?"

He smiled impishly. "I wanted it to be a surprise."

By now we had reached a small theater called the Vanishing Act Room, and Perry guided me to a crimson plush chair. "I—uh—I've got to get backstage. The show's going to start any minute now. I hope you enjoy it. I'll see you afterward, OK?"

"Sure," I said, taking a seat as he scurried behind the heavy blue velvet curtain.

What's going on here? I wondered. *This isn't how the fantasy is supposed to go. Perry is supposed to be here in the audience with me, not be part of the entertainment.* My disappointment in the sudden turn of events made me question Perry's motives for asking me here in the first place. Did he really care for me, or did he just want to show off? *It's so hard to know whether or not you can trust a guy*, I thought.

At least I didn't have time to dwell on this unsettling issue. A few seconds after I'd taken my seat, the lights dimmed and a gray-haired, tuxedo-clad man walked across the stage as the audience applauded.

"Good evening, ladies and gentlemen, and welcome to the House of Cards. Tonight, we're proud to bring you . . ."

I only half heard the opening introductions, which seemed to take forever. But I heard enough to figure out that Perry was second on the bill, which meant that he'd be back to join me for the three remaining acts. I was glad for that. If there's anything that makes me uncomfortable, it's sitting alone in an audience. It's hard for me to relax and enjoy whatever I'm watching if I don't have someone—anyone—to enjoy it with.

Even though it had been a shock to learn that Perry would be performing that night, I was anxious to see what kind of act he did. It was only fair that I see his performance, since he'd already seen mine. Ignoring the three-hundred-pound man squeezed into the chair next to me, I concentrated on watching the first performer, a comedy magician whose act consisted mostly of making giant-sized sponge balls appear and disappear while he told a story. I had the idea he thought the story was funny, but no one in the Vanishing Act Room found him amusing. I didn't either, but I forced myself to chuckle occasionally because I knew how hard it was to face an audience and I felt kind of sorry for the guy.

About halfway through his act, my concentration wandered from the stage to my left foot. It was throbbing; the thin leather strap of my shoe was cutting across my ankle like a wire. I'd felt it all the time I'd been with Perry, but it hadn't bothered me then. Now I was in agony. Although I desperately wanted to take the shoe off, I didn't dare; I was afraid I'd never be able to get it back on again. *This is the last time I wear heels*, I grumbled silently as I attempted to force my thoughts back to the stage.

Finally the comic had the good sense to leave and make way for Perry. I was surprised when, during the break, the girl I'd figured was Perry's sister came out and put up an old-fashioned sign on an easel announcing: Ingram the Invincible. She looked dazzling and very sexy in a tight-fitting silver lamé leotard and mesh tights that looked as if they could have come from Frederick's. She wore black stiletto heels, too, and I couldn't help wondering if her feet ever hurt her.

Then the gray-haired master of ceremonies came out again and announced: "Ladies and gentlemen. I present Perry Ingram the Invincible and his lovely assistant, Lana Feliciano."

The stage blacked out—which is what I wished I could have done at that moment. They have different last names, I kept repeating to myself, and short of their being half brother and sister, which I thought unlikely, that could mean only one thing: they were a couple. Remembering the kiss Lana gave him that afternoon and Bert's snide remark about Perry's girls, I felt sick to my stomach. Why had Perry brought me here? What kind of cruel boy was he? How much did I really know about him, anyway? I wondered, staring blankly at his routine through eyes blurry with tears.

I probably would have sat like that for the rest of the night, letting my tears block my vision, but the bursts of applause made me wipe them away and see what all the fuss was about. I cleared my eyes just in time to see Perry reach into a large square box that *she* was holding and pull out a never-ending line of silk handkerchiefs. It didn't look like a big deal to me, but the fat man next to me was whispering "Wonderful, wonderful" over and over to the man next to him.

When the applause died down, Lana took the box away and returned with a table with a pan on top of it. Perry lifted the lid and showed the audience there was nothing inside. Then he took a piece of paper out of his pocket. Lana handed him a match, and he set the paper on fire, then placed it inside the pan and covered the leaping flame with the lid. Silently he waved his arms and upon removing the lid revealed two cooing doves.

I had to admit it: I was impressed. I kept looking back and forth between the doves and Perry's face to see if I could figure out how he had done it. Perry took in the applause, acknowledging it graciously with a slight bow of his head before moving on to his next trick.

While Lana took the doves off the stage, Perry reached into a back pocket and took out a long silk streamer. He held it out to the audience, showing that it was just a streamer. But somehow, after about the fourth or fifth run of his hands over the silk, a dove miraculously appeared. And then another one.

I found myself clapping so hard my hands began to hurt more than my feet. No matter what kind of trickery he had used to get me to come here, he was an outstanding magician and a super performer, and I had to give him credit for that.

Then my mood was spoiled when Lana came

back on stage, this time with a table and a cage. Perry placed the two doves inside and covered the cage with a large black cloth. Then he slowly lifted the cage off the table toward the front of the stage. As he got near the edge, he threw the cage into the air—but all that fell to the ground was the cloth.

The hush that had come over the audience was soon replaced with thunderous applause. "He's great," I heard one woman in the row behind me whisper.

"I've seen him before," said the man on the other side of her. "He gets better all the time."

Perry bowed deeply to the audience before exiting stage left. Almost immediately, he returned with Lana on his arm. That's when I stopped clapping.

The audience calmed down as the master of ceremonies came on to introduce the next act. I grew anxious, though, as I rehearsed in my mind what I was going to say to Perry when he came out to join me. I thought of starting out with "So how's your girlfriend?" but discarded it as being too obvious and rude. No, it would be better for me to be cool and sophisticated and shrug off the other girl as if she didn't matter.

Fat chance, I concluded. I was too nervous and upset to be cool and sophisticated.

By the time the third act was over, Perry

still hadn't come out. He probably had to put away the doves, I rationalized, amazed that in my state of mind I was able to come up with such a reasonable excuse. But when the fourth performer began to take his bows and there was still no Perry, I became seriously concerned. It didn't take that long to tend to a couple of birds, I told myself. *But it might take this long to tend to Lana,* an inner voice cried out.

That thought was more than I could stand. Between the hurt of being stood up and the physical pain of my throbbing feet, I couldn't bear to stay there a minute longer. Perry was rejecting me, and it was more than I could handle. If he was going to stand me up, I'd have to show him I didn't care. As soon as the fourth act was over, I got up and hobbled out of the room.

I made a wrong turn somewhere and found myself at a dead-end in a hallway, facing a hologram of a magician levitating a woman in mid-air. Making a quick turn, I hurried back down the hall and stumbled into a game room where a combination of calliope music and video bleeps left me feeling even more disoriented than ever. Fortunately someone there was about to leave, and I followed him to the front exit.

I was never so happy to get out of a place in my life. I vowed that this was the last time I'd ever try to live out one of my fantasies. Reality was no fun at all.

Chapter Five

It was only eight o'clock, a full half hour before Sara and Caroline were due, but here I was already, sitting on the edge of one of the planters at the front of my house, waiting for the girls so we could go running. I wasn't being particularly diligent; I just needed to get out of the house. I'd been awake for over two hours, and I was more than a little restless.

Sighing, I looked down at my Nike-clad feet. The pain from the night before was gone, but I wished the same could be said for the nearly constant ache I felt in my heart. I still couldn't believe I had misread Perry's intentions so badly; I couldn't believe that all that the shy, soft-spoken boy wanted was another loving fan to applaud him and his beautiful girlfriend.

Shaking my head, I tried to erase all thoughts of Perry from my consciousness. I knew that the first thing Sara and Caroline would want to talk about was my date, and I just wasn't ready to share the details with them. I still felt foolish about my mistake, and the last thing I wanted to hear was one of Caroline's I-told-you-so's about the immaturity of today's teenage male, or one of Sara's too cheery better-luck-next-time's. Maybe the next day, when the wound would be a little less painful, I'd confide in them, but for the moment I'd pretend the night had been terrific and hope that that would satisfy their curiosity. Just to be on the safe side, I'd applied an extra heavy layer of cover-up on the circles under my eyes. I'd noticed them this morning after having stumbled to the bath-room after too few hours of fitful sleep, and the last thing I needed was for the girls to notice them, too.

Mom had always told me that a foolproof way to lift one's spirits was to concentrate on happy thoughts. Closing my eyes, I found myself drifting back to less complicated times in Michigan with Gilly. It still amazed me that my mind would automatically flash to him whenever I needed a lift. But then Gilly Edwards had always made me smile during the year and a half we dated. It was Gilly who first showed me how to do a trick shuffle and Gilly whom I'd later impressed by learning how to do card tricks that even he didn't know. Gilly went on to become my biggest fan, happy to let me teach him all I'd taught myself about magic. In return, Gilly introduced me to a world where feelings I'd never imagined before were awakened inside me. He was as gentle and caring a boyfriend as any girl could want, and when I had to tell him I was moving away, we spent evening after evening crying in each other's arms.

We had promised we'd continue our relationship by mail and long-distance phone calls, but as I was to discover, a promise like that is nearly impossible to keep. The last time I'd heard from him had been Christmas, and I'd since found out from my best friend in Michigan that he'd begun to date other girls—just as I had gone out with other boys. He was only a memory now. Even so I still got goose bumps thinking about Gilly, and I could feel the corners of my mouth starting to turn upward.

"Hey, Nicki, I didn't know you'd taken up meditating," Sara said.

Opening my eyes I found myself back in California, facing my new best girlfriend. "Morning, chum," I said cheerily, fixing the waistband on my sweat pants as I rose to meet her.

"You're in a good mood this morning," Sara said. "Thinking about last night, huh?"

"Wouldn't you like to know," I said, adding quickly, "Let's go get Caroline."

A few minutes later the three of us were

jogging down to the corner. I could tell Sara was dying to know about the date, and sure enough as we crossed the street, she turned to me and remarked, "Must have had a hot time last night, I'll bet."

Ignoring the comment, I continued to jog nonchalantly down the block.

"Think she'll tell us about it?" Caroline wondered aloud.

I fell into step with the others. "It was an *interesting* evening," I decided to tell them. "I'll tell you more about it later. Where are we jogging to today?"

"To the junior high and back, mystery lady," said Sara.

"That all? Sounds like you had a tiring night, too."

"Oh, you know what happens when a bunch of girls get together to party. Talk, talk, talk. We must have spent a good three hours rating Paul Ramus alone. You should have been there."

Paul Ramus was a new transfer student who'd immediately risen to the top of the most-desirable list at Jacaranda High. "I thought you guys were going to talk about other things than boys," I said, huffing. We'd only gone two blocks so far, but the sun was an awful lot hotter than it had seemed from my front steps. I wished I'd brought along my sweat band.

"That resolution lasted about five minutes," Caroline put in.

"C'mon, Nicki, when did you ever hear of girls getting together and not talking about boys?" Sara added. "The best part was when Marcy took out this old quiz she'd found in a magazine about how to pick your perfect match. It was so funny!"

"Yeah. According to the results, Sara's dream guy is six-five and likes chamber music and green vegetables," Caroline said.

"And you know how I hate broccoli," Sara chimed in. "But Caroline here didn't make out any better." She grinned at Caroline, then said to me, "Let me see, if I remember right, the quiz said she prefers jock types who like to work with their hands."

"I don't know, Sara. That sounds like your type to me," I said. "Speaking of which, how's Carl?"

"As blond and beautiful as ever." We paused at an intersection to wait for the light to change. Sara turned back to me. "We've got to get Marcy to give you the quiz."

"Why?" asked Caroline. "I know the answer to that one already. She likes guys with magic fingers."

The hurt of the night before immediately flashed to the forefront of my consciousness.

"You think you always know everything, Caroline," I grumbled testily.

"Hey, what'd I say?" she asked. "Did I say something wrong?"

Why was it that one romantic reference to Perry put me back into a foul mood? "No," I lied, turning away. "Let's cross this street, OK? I've got to get back home soon." I raced to the other side just before the light changed, and my friends had to run at full speed to catch up with me.

"What's gotten into you?" Sara asked as we slowed down to a jogging pace again. Moving closer to get a good look at me, she added, "Hey, what's that stuff on your face? You haven't been crying, have you?"

My makeup was running. "No," I said, wiping my cheeks. Beige streaks now stained my hands.

"Something's wrong, though. I can tell," Sara said.

"Maybe she doesn't want to talk about it," Caroline said.

"Is that it, Nicki? Is something bothering you? We're your friends, kid. If you've got a problem, we've got a problem. You can tell us."

I slowed to a walk, surprised by the genuine concern in her voice. "You sure you want to hear this?"

"If you're in trouble, I want to help you,"

Sara said, draping her arm across my shoulders. "It's about last night, isn't it?"

I nodded. "Nothing happened the way I thought it would," I said, forgetting the one magic moment Perry and I had had together. "Ingram the Invincible was more like Ingram the Intolerable. He stood me up."

"He didn't show up?" Sara asked, shocked.

"No, he was there. But he had me sit in the audience while he performed. I didn't mind that—in fact, he was very good—except that he had to go and parade his girlfriend out there in front of me as his assistant."

"Now why would he have invited you out if he's already got a girlfriend?" Sara asked.

"As a courtesy to a fellow magician, probably."

"That can't be all," Sara said. "When you called me yesterday afternoon, you said he seemed really happy to see you again."

"At the time I thought so. Even after this girl came around in the magic store. I thought she was his sister. But she's not. And then I waited through two acts after his, and he didn't come back into the audience. He was probably so wrapped up with her that he forgot about me."

"Maybe he had to put all his magic stuff away," Sara said.

"How long does that take?" I argued. "Besides, he never even told me about the show. When he'd asked me to the club, he told me we were going . . . to . . . see—" I stopped in my tracks, overcome with a horrible thought.

"See what, Nicki?" Caroline asked.

"I don't believe it," I said, wiping away more of my runny makeup.

Sara looked confused. "Believe what, Nicki?"

"I was so mad at the way the night was turning out, so surprised to see that girl there, so upset with my sore foot—"

"Your foot?" Sara interrupted.

"Never mind that," I continued. "I was so wrapped up in my hurt I totally forgot he said he was going to take me to see a close-up magician . . . *after* his show. Boy, what a jerk."

"Yeah, he should have been more specific about when he was going to meet you," Caroline said.

"No, not him—*me.* I'm the stupid one. He probably came out into the audience after the whole show was over. He must think *I* stood *him* up!"

"But what about the girlfriend?" Sara asked. "How does she fit into all this?"

"I don't know. Unless . . ." I took a deep breath, the memory of how Perry had seemed to care about me in the early part of the evening coming back to me with full force. "Maybe I was jumping to conclusions about her, too. Maybe she's not his girlfriend after all."

"I think there's only one way you can find out," Sara said.

"How?"

"Call him up."

"I can't do that!" I cried. The thought made me so jumpy that I started us off at a slow jog again.

"Why not? You know his name and where he lives, so you could look his number up in the phone book. And if worse came to worst, you could always ask Greg for it."

"I don't know," I hedged. "What if I'm wrong and he doesn't want to hear from me?"

"That's what I like to hear, real positive thinking." Sara snorted.

"Hey, don't be so hard on her," Caroline said. "It's tough to call a boy."

"You can't think about that," Sara said. "Or you'll never get near the phone. You've got to think positive, Nicki, think that your gut reactions about Perry are right. You two probably had one gigantic communication gap last night. But you'll never know whether I'm right unless you talk to him."

"I suppose," I said. "I'll call him as soon as I get home."

Chapter Six

Sara was right: I had to call Perry and get this whole thing straightened out. I very well might have jumped to the wrong conclusion about him at the House of Cards, and I could probably resolve the entire situation with one phone call.

I should have known better than to think things would work out so simply.

Five minutes after I returned home, I got Perry's number from information. That was easy, but calling him was another story. I'd never had any qualms about picking up the phone to talk to Nick or to Dale, my biology lab partner, or to any boy I was just friends with. I guess I felt so nervous now because I knew Perry had the potential to be more than just a friend. One wrong word during the phone conversation and that potential could fly out the window for good.

After fifteen minutes of trying to muster up my nerve, I picked up the phone to dial but froze after pressing the first three numbers. What would I say? "Hi, Perry. This is the girl who walked out on you last night. How are you?" Or, "Perry, I would have waited all night for you to come back to where I was sitting, but I had to go home with a bad case of swollen feet."

Everything that raced through my mind sounded stupid to me, so I put down the phone. Then I tried to calm myself with some comforting thoughts, and I came to the conclusion that Perry was probably just as confused about our date as I was. Actually, he was probably so confused that *he* would be calling *me* to straighten things out. It would only be a matter of time, I figured, before I'd be answering his phone call. I checked the kitchen clock and found that it was only nine-fifteen—it was too early to call him, anyway. Feeling somewhat relieved, I poured myself some bran flakes and put up a pot of coffee for my still sleeping parents. Chris, I decided, could fend for himself when he bothered to get out of bed.

After I finished breakfast, I went to the family room to look over my new book of card tricks. This was my favorite room in the house, much more comfortable than my bedroom, which, after seven months, still had that just-moved-in look to it. The family room was bright and inviting. A skylight bathed the walls with natural light and gave life to the numerous plants Mom and I had picked out from the local nursery. One wall of the wood-paneled room held the entertainment system, including the fanciest stereo you could imagine. I turned the radio on and tuned in my favorite station. Then I put on the headphones so I could turn the volume up without waking anyone.

I took out a brand-new deck of cards and plopped down on the carpet against the sofa. Then I turned to the first chapter in my new book and read over the first group of tricks.

Five minutes later I put the book down with dismay. This wasn't going to be easy, I realized. All of the tricks involved complicated palming and shuffling tricks I hadn't yet mastered. "But I guess there's no better time than now to learn," I said to myself. Picking up the book again, I flipped to the final section, where the techniques were explained.

In the next two and a half hours I practically wore out the deck trying to do a Faro shuffle. That's a maneuver where the deck is divided in half and all the cards interlock perfectly. When it's done right, it's possible to keep track of any individual card, while to the audience it looks like the cards are being shuffled into confusion. But let me tell you, it's very hard to get it right. At one point while I was practicing, I slipped, and the cards flew all over the room. The next time I shuffled, the cards went only as far as the TV set. *I'm making progress*, I thought. As Sara had told me, I had to start looking at the positive side of things. I finally got to the point where I was able to complete the shuffle successfully, but whether I'd ever be able to do it without looking like I was trying to do something sneaky was another story entirely.

A short while later, Chris popped his head into the room, and seeing what I was up to, he decided to bother me. I took off the headphones to hear what he was saying.

"Hey, whatcha doing?" Chris asked. "New tricks? Let me see."

My right hand was beginning to cramp, and my fingers felt as if they'd never function again. "No way!" I said, putting down the cards. "Petersen the Peerless has petered out for the day."

The other, littler Petersen wasn't finished pestering me, though. "How about an old trick, then?" he pleaded. "Like the Six-Card shuffle. OK, Nicki? Please?"

Boy, did I hate it when he pulled his doe-eyed act on me! I'd first noticed this trick of his last summer when he was sick with mononucleosis. I'd spend hours entertaining him with tricks to keep him from being bored, and just when I'd finish what I'd hope would be the last one, he'd open his big blue eyes extra wide and stare at me pathetically. Naturally I'd feel so sorry for him my heart would melt, and I'd continue doing the tricks until I'd performed every one I knew. I hadn't really minded at the time, but the worst part was that now he knew he'd discovered how to get to me, and he'd put on that doleful look every time he wanted something. I felt that Chris was getting too old to pull that kind of an act, yet I couldn't keep myself from falling for it every time. "All right," I said. "Just this one. That's all."

"Terrific," he said, falling onto the rug opposite me.

"First you've got to turn around a second while I get ready," I said, pulling down the sleeves of my sweat shirt.

Half a minute later he whined, "Ready yet?"

"OK, you can turn around now."

Quickly I fanned out the small pile of cards in my hand. "See, kid, it's really just a simple little thing. First I take these six cards in my right hand and count them out like this: one, two, three, four, five, six. Now I'm going to count off three cards and give them to you. How many cards do I have left?"

"Three!" he cried.

"Let's see." I counted off the cards again.

"One, two, three, four, five, six. You're wrong. I've got six cards. Looks like you can't count too well."

"How'd you do that?" he asked, amazed.

"Just lucky, I guess." I shrugged.

"C'mon, there's more to it than that."

"Let's try it again and see what happens." I gave my brother three more cards and began counting out the remaining cards in my hand, "One, two"—but froze when the phone rang. Someone in the kitchen picked it up on the second ring, and I held my breath waiting to see if it was for me. When no sounds came from the kitchen, I continued the count: "Three, four, five—"

"Nicki, telephone!" my mother shouted.

"Coming," I shouted back.

"There's a phone in here, stupid." My brother laughed.

"You wouldn't understand. I'm taking it in my bedroom." I jumped up quickly, and the six cards I still had hidden up my sleeve fell down behind me.

"So that's where the cards come from," Chris said as I closed the family room door behind me.

My heart was thumping furiously. The call had to be from Perry, of course. I ran to my bedroom and picked up the extension. Letting out a breath, I purred into the phone, "Hello."

"So what happened?"

"Oh, it's you, Sara." I tugged at my hair in disappointment.

"Who'd you think it was? Superman?"

"I was hoping it would be Perry," I said glumly.

"So did you speak to him? What did he say?" Sara asked excitedly.

"Nothing."

"He sure is a quiet one, isn't he?"

"He didn't say anything because I didn't speak to him yet."

"You didn't? Why not?"

"I thought I'd try him later this afternoon."

"Don't chicken out, Nicki. I'll call you later."

The line went dead. "The least you can do is say goodbye," I said, slamming down the receiver.

I still had faith that Perry would call before the day was out. To occupy myself I went back into the family room, where my brother was playing solitaire with my cards. Without his even having to ask, I began to practice more magic tricks for him. Every time I finished a trick I'd glance at the beige Touch-Tone.

But no Perry.

After dinner I resigned myself to taking the plunge and calling him. I went to my room, closed the door (wishing it had a lock), and, with trembling fingers, made the call. On the fourth ring a woman answered.

"Hello, uh, um, is Perry there?"

"No," the woman said. "Hold on a moment, won't you?" Then she put down the phone. I heard some noise on the other end, and soon the woman came back on. "Perry's over at Lana's, but he should be back in about an hour. Would you like to leave a message?"

"No, no message," I said. I hung up quickly.

For the longest time I sat on my bed with the phone in my lap and stared at the wild flowers on the wallpaper-covered wall opposite me as if I were in a trance. But the reality was too clear to ignore. There was no denying it now. There could be only one reason why Perry would be spending the evening with Lana. I winced in pain.

It's not fair, I thought over and over. After all this time in California, I'd finally found a boy I could like—and he had to have a girlfriend.

Chapter Seven

"Nicki, telephone!" Chris shouted from the kitchen the following evening.

"I'm right here," I said, walking in from the dining room where I'd been clearing the dinner dishes. I picked up the receiver from where Chris had dropped it and shot him a "get lost" look. He stuck his tongue out at me as he stalked off into the dining room.

"Nicki's talking to a boy, Nicki's talking to a boy," he sang teasingly through the door.

Suddenly my nervous system went into temporary shutdown. *A boy! Uh-oh.* I had the panicky feeling that this wasn't a social call from Nick or Dale. Somehow I managed to lift the receiver to my mouth and whisper, "Hello?"

"Nicki?" The voice on the other end seemed unsure, too. "Nicki, this is Perry."

"Hi," I said with a little more enthusiasm.

It was so good to hear his voice! After Saturday night I'd been sure that I'd never hear it again, and hearing it now brought up memories of the night we'd met. I couldn't let my own voice betray my pleasure, though, I realized, especially since I didn't know why he was calling. I'd have to hold back my feelings till I was sure of his intentions. Trying to sound as cool as I could, I adopted my most laid-back tone and said, "What's up, Perry?"

"Nicki, I have a question. Did you call me last night?" he asked.

"Yes," I admitted, wondering how he knew and worrying what he might think of me now.

"Yeah, Mom told me a girl called. Listen, I—um—was wondering what happened to you the other night. I thought we were going to meet after the show."

My coolness evaporated at the mention of that horrible night at the House of Cards.

"So did I," I blurted out. "Only I didn't count on Ingram the Invincible being Ingram the Inconsiderate."

"Inconsiderate? Huh? What did I do?"

"Well, for starters, there was your act. What was the idea of not telling me you were the main attraction? What kind of surprise is that to lay on someone you hardly know? And then plopping me in the middle of the room between a fat slob and a prissy old lady who wheezed all night—great company. But I didn't mind that as long as I knew you'd be coming back after your act to take me to see the close-up guy I'd come to see in the first place. But when you didn't bother showing up . . . well, how much is a girl supposed to take?"

What was I doing? Here was the moment I'd been waiting for—and I was positively blowing it in the biggest way possible. I could hear the venom in my voice as I ranted and raved, but once I'd opened my mouth the words had tumbled out in an uncontrollable torrent. The hurt I'd suffered at the House of Cards had been so overwhelming that I just couldn't hold back my anger and frustration.

After I'd finished yelling, I waited. There was silence for a very long time. "Perry?" I finally asked tentatively, wondering if he'd ever want to say another word to me after my outburst. "Are you still there?"

"Yeah. Are you finished?"

"I think so."

"I don't suppose you'd be interested in my explanation."

"Try me. I imagine a magician as inventive as you could come up with some pretty clever excuses," I said, slightly mollified, but still wary.

"Would you settle for the truth?"

The truth? Now that I had calmed down a

bit I figured that Perry had to have a reasonable explanation for his actions, or he wouldn't have called. "Sure, Perry, go ahead," I said quietly.

"What happened was that after I saw you at the magic shop, I got a call from the club asking me to substitute for somebody who got sick. I thought about calling you and telling you not to come, but I changed my mind when it occurred to me that maybe you'd want to see my act. Looks like I guessed wrong."

I couldn't tell if it was only my wishful thinking or not, but he sounded terribly disappointed about what had happened. Now I really regretted my wild outburst. "You didn't guess wrong, Perry," I said. "But you should have told me." I hoped he could hear the regret in my voice. "I didn't mean to come on so strong before. I'm sorry."

"That's OK, Nicki. I should have been more clear about the plans. But I liked the idea of surprising you—that is, until I came out after the show and saw you were gone. You must have left right after I went backstage, huh?"

"Why, no, Perry. We made plans to meet after your show, and I had no intention of standing you up."

"Then what happened?"

"That's what I was going to explain before I let my emotions get the best of me. It'll probably sound stupid, I know, but it's the truth. Sometimes I can get really fidgety and nervous sitting in a crowded room with strangers. I waited for you after your act, but when you didn't come out, I thought you were standing me up. I—I didn't know what else to do, so I left." I couldn't bring myself to tell Perry the other, more important reason I had left—not then, at least.

"I'm sorry to hear that," he said. "You should have come backstage."

"I didn't know I could," I said. Inside I was thinking that even if I'd known, I wouldn't have had any desire to go back there and tangle with Lana.

"Yeah, well, I guess I should have told you. Afterward I realized that I hadn't told you I had to stay backstage until the whole show was over. You must have gotten bored out there. Will you forgive me, Nicki?"

"No apologies necessary," I said, relieved to hear the sincerity in his voice. "Besides, how could I be bored watching Ingram the Outstanding?"

"That's Invincible," he corrected me.

"Anyway, you were really super."

"Thanks," he said. "I've been working on the dove routines for a couple of months. That was only the second time I've performed them in public."

"Well, you fooled me. You looked like an old pro up there."

"Thanks again," he said, sounding more at ease now that the subject had shifted to magic. "I must have practiced each one of those bits at least a thousand times. You should have seen the first time I tried to hide a dove. I nearly decapitated it."

"Really? I thought I was the only one who had trouble learning new moves. Just yesterday I tried a new shuffle, and I thought my hands were going to die of fatigue."

"It happens to everyone," Perry said. After a short pause he hesitantly added, "Are you ready to learn more about magic?"

So he still wanted to give me that private lesson! A shudder of delight raced through me at the thought of seeing him again and making another stab at developing a relationship with him. "You bet," I said.

Perry's response, though, was not at all what I had in mind. "Well, next Saturday morning the House of Cards is having a workshop for new magicians. I'm going to be leading it, and I thought you might want to come."

"Saturday! I don't know if I can make it," I said evasively. If I was only going to be another face in the crowd to him, I had no desire to go.

"I hope you'll come. It starts at nine-thirty at the club. I'll be going over a wide variety of techniques, but afterward we could get together, and I could help you with your card problem."

So there might be hope for us after all! I began to wonder how important it was to Perry that I be there. So far he hadn't said a word about Lana, and I certainly wasn't going to mention her name. "Well, I think I might be able to make it," I told him, willing to take the chance that she wouldn't be around.

"Well," Perry said haltingly, "I'm glad."

I was glad, too. This workshop thing had to mean that Perry was still interested in me. But the real proof would come on Saturday, when I could see for myself exactly where I fit into Ingram the Invincible's plans.

Chapter Eight

It's amazing how one phone call can change a person's entire mood. As soon as I got off the phone with Perry, I called Sara; after she'd analyzed every one of Perry's words, she convinced me that I'd been given a second chance after nearly blowing everything with him the other night.

"Perry must really like you," Sara said, after I'd admitted that I'd jumped to the wrong conclusion about his intentions. "If this Lana person really meant a lot to him, he wouldn't be bothering with you at all. Either that or he's a real uncaring slime."

"Well, if he is a rat, then I'm the worst judge of character in the world," I assured her.

My good spirits lasted all the way into the following day. I shrugged off one of Chris's temper tantrums the next morning at breakfast and discovered to my surprise that he calmed down rather quickly after he realized I was ignoring him. I made a mental note to remember that for the future.

I didn't get upset, either, when I walked into a surprise quiz on *Romeo and Juliet* in English lit. or when Mrs. Kennedy made me do sit-ups in PE until I thought my stomach was going to burst. I was able to get through the agony by thinking *Perry, Perry,* every time I pulled myself up.

After I showered I hurried out of school and headed over to the Santa Rosa Street School Reading Center and my weekly volunteer session. During the three-block walk, I ran my fingers through my still damp hair, trying to make it fluff out a little. Usually my shoulder-length, tapered hair falls in bouncy layers around my face, but when I have to let it dry in the open air I can't do too much to prevent it from hanging limply.

It wasn't long before I reached the school. I walked into the center, waving hello to Mrs. Radner, the reading teacher. She was the kind of caring, motherly type of teacher I hoped to be someday. That is, if I still wanted to be a teacher by the time I got out of college. My guidance counselor had suggested that I work at the reading center to help me decide if I was really interested in teaching. Some days, when one of the kids would have a breakthrough, I'd feel terrific and think that there was no more rewarding job in the world than teaching. But on the days when no real progress was made, I'd feel inadequate and decide I'd probably be better off doing something less emotionally upsetting.

After I'd passed by several other volunteers from my school, I took a seat next to one of my students, a cute little boy named Mitchell, who was already at work at one of the reading machines.

"How are you doing today, Mitchell?" I asked pleasantly.

"Fine," he answered, still staring at the screen.

Typical Mitchell behavior, I thought. In the three months I'd been working there, I'd never been able to get a decent conversation going with him. But that really didn't matter, since the main reason Mitchell was at the reading center was to learn how to read better. Already he had made remarkable progress, and I felt that it would be just a matter of weeks before he'd be reading as well as the rest of his third-grade classmates.

"Let's hear what the machine has to say today," I told him.

"OK." Mitchell paused and began to read. "Pi-pigeons are har-hardy birds that live all over the wo-world. They get al-long with lit-little care. There are . . ."

Yawn, I thought. Couldn't they have programmed something more interesting? I had a feeling all these kids would be reading better if the stuff they had to figure out wasn't designed to put them to sleep first. "You're doing beautifully, Mitchell," I told the boy, who continued reading. "Keep going. I'm going to check on Mary Beth now."

I turned my chair to the freckled-faced girl to my right. "Mary Beth, how come your machine isn't turned on?" The girl was bouncing a tiny, bright orange ball against the darkened video screen.

"I was waiting for you," Mary Beth answered, her chin stuck out defiantly.

"You know you're supposed to start without me," I said, for what may have been the tenth time since I had begun working with the nine-year-old girl. Unlike Mitchell, Mary Beth had a hard time concentrating on her reading; she often made up excuses for why she couldn't decipher the letters before her.

"It's no fun doing it alone." Mary Beth turned away from me and started playing with the ball again.

"Well, I'm here now, Mary Beth. Would you turn on the machine?" I asked nicely.

"You didn't say please," she answered, rising slightly to catch a high bounce.

"Would you *please* turn on the machine?" I said a little more forcefully. I could feel myself losing patience fast. It looked like it was going to be one of those days.

"No!" Mary Beth said.

"Why not?"

"I don't feel like it." *Bounce.*

"Turn on the machine, Mary Beth." *Bounce. Bounce.*

"Maybe I will, maybe I won't," the girl responded. Tired of throwing the ball at the screen, she began to bounce it on the floor between her and me.

"Now give me the ball and turn on the machine. If you don't do what I say, I'll have to call Mrs. Radner."

But Mary Beth just ignored me and continued to play with the ball. I could see I needed to take a different approach.

"If you don't want to hand me the ball, I'm just going to have to take it." Before Mary Beth's startled eyes, I seized the ball in mid bounce and palmed it in my right hand. A split second later it was nowhere to be found, vanished into thin air. Or so Mary Beth thought.

"Hey, where's my ball?" she cried. Her shout was loud enough to make Mrs. Radner look up in our direction. The teacher watched as I went into my explanation.

Feigning ignorance, I shrugged and said, "I don't know."

"You took my ball. You made it disappear! Give it back."

"Maybe I will, and maybe I won't," I said. Noting Mary Beth's expression of hurt and puzzlement, I added, "Tell you what. I can make the ball come back, but only if you read to me first."

"That's blackmail!" the girl said, stunned. She sat in silence for a minute before she meekly flicked the switch of the machine. "How much do I have to read?"

"Just one paragraph. Then answer the questions at the end. And *then* I'll give you the ball back."

I guess Mary Beth really wanted her toy because even though she made a lot of mistakes, she got through the material much faster than she ever had before.

As I got ready to leave, Mrs. Radner motioned for me to come to her desk. "I liked the way you handled Mary Beth today," she said. "How were you able to get that ball away from her? I tried to take it before you got here, and she practically threw a tantrum."

"It was magic, Mrs. Radner."

"I'll say. I often don't know what to do with that girl."

"No, I mean it was real magic. I palmed the ball and pocketed it in my blazer before she had a chance to react. It was an act of desperation of my part, but I think it worked."

"Where did you learn how to do that, Nicki?"

"Back in Michigan. I do some card tricks and stuff, too."

"Really?" Mrs. Radner leaned her elbows against her metal desk. "I could use a trick like that every now and again."

"I could teach you, if you'd like," I offered.

"I don't think so." Mrs. Radner shook her head. "I'm too old for that. But I think there is something you can do for me. Nicki, these kids work so hard in here, and their progress comes in such small steps it's often difficult for them to see it. I think it would be a good idea to give them some encouragement for their work. How would you like to perform some of your magic for them sometime?"

"I'd love to," I said without a moment's hesitation. "I've never done my tricks for little kids, but I bet it would be fun."

"Good. Why don't we plan on it for around the end of next month, right before Easter vacation?"

"Sounds good to me." I began to walk away but then turned back as a thought popped into my head. "Mrs. Radner, how about a real magic show with big illusions and costumes and the works!"

She looked at me skeptically. "I don't know, Nicki. The school certainly doesn't have the budget for anything that elaborate."

"But what if I could do it for free?"

"I think that would be a pretty tall order for a girl like you."

"Well, I'm not promising Doug Henning or anyone like that. But what if I could arrange for a real, full-fledged magician to perform along with me?"

"Well, Nicki," Mrs. Radner said, "if you can arrange it—at no cost to the school that is—I suppose it will be all right with me."

"Wonderful," I said. Whistling happily as I walked out the door, I set to thinking about how I could get help from the one person who could make this magic show possible.

Chapter Nine

As I drove to the House of Cards the next Saturday morning, I felt a mixture of excitement and dread. I hadn't spoken to Perry since he'd called me, and during the week I'd been seesawing between feeling that he really liked me and feeling that he was just being nice to me because I was another magician.

Sara wasn't helping matters any. On Wednesday she told me to be really aggressive and to demand a date with Perry when I saw him or to cross him off my list for good. But on Thursday she changed her mind and told me I'd be better off playing it cool and aloof. By Friday Sara had had a big fight with Carl and suggested that the best thing I could do was to stick to my magic and to forget Perry, and all boys for that matter, entirely.

On Saturday I didn't bother to call Sara. It

94

would have been too early anyway. I got up at six because I wanted to take extra care with my appearance. I kept my hot rollers on my head for an extra ten minutes and then carefully fluffed out my hair with my fingertips. My fingernails took on a neater look, too, with the new nail polish I'd bought especially for this day. My nails weren't very long, and I wished I could let them grow as long as Sara's, but they had to be kept short so as not to mess up my card tricks. But that day they looked very pretty, and I was sure that Perry would notice when I performed my tricks for him.

I made the turn off the San Diego Freeway onto Sunset Boulevard and drove carefully up the winding road toward the club.

During the day the valets in their magicians' costumes were nowhere to be found. I parked the car myself and made my way up the steps, glad that today I didn't have to wear heels. When I reached the entrance, I followed a redheaded boy into the club and down the steps to the basement where the workshop was being held.

The room was all set up, with a long table at the front and rows of metal folding chairs all the way to the back. Behind the table were a blackboard and a bulletin board filled with notices of upcoming events and personal appearances. I stepped into the room and looked for an empty seat not too close to the front. It was only nine-fifteen, but the basement was already half full. Perry was sitting at the table talking to two boys and didn't notice that I'd arrived. I was the only girl in the room, and while I was glad that there was no sign of Lana, I found that being in a room full of boys was a strangely unsettling experience.

Before I could sit down, though, Perry spotted me and called out my name.

"Nicki, glad you could come," he said. He leaned away from the two boys and indicated that he wanted me to come up to see him.

So far so good, I thought. I jumped up and joined him, unable to keep a big smile from appearing on my face. "How are you, Perry?" I asked, trying to keep my voice even yet friendly.

"Just fine," he said. "A little nervous, maybe, but I think I've got that under control."

"Why should you be nervous?"

"This is only my second workshop. Until last year I used to be one of them," he said, pointing at the seated boys. "But the board of directors has been pleased with my progress this year, and they think I have something to offer the younger students."

Plunging ahead before I could stop myself, I said, "Speaking of having something to offer, something came up this week that I thought you might be interested in. A teacher at the reading center where I do volunteer work asked me to put on a magic show. I was wondering if you would be interested in performing there."

Perry shook his head. "Sorry, Nicki, I can't," he said decisively.

My mouth fell open. I had been so sure he'd say yes! "But you've got to!" I pleaded.

Perry examined his fingernails and fidgeted. "I'm awfully busy," he said, unable to look me directly in the eye.

"But, Perry," I continued in desperation, "you wouldn't have to do anything too elaborate. It'd only take an hour or so—and the kids would appreciate it so much. Isn't there any way you can make it?"

He thought for a long moment. "This month is impossible, Nicki. I'm sorry."

"But it's not until next month!"

"When?"

"I'm not sure of the exact date yet. Sometime around the end of the month."

"The last week?" he wondered.

"Yes."

He looked up at me as he seemed to reconsider. "OK," he said finally. "If it's the last week in March, I'll do it."

I wanted to hug him in gratitude but held myself back. "Thank you," I said, grinning.

He smiled back at me. "How old are the kids?"

"Eight and nine, mostly."

"Great. That age makes the best audience."

I couldn't help myself, I had to ask. "Will you be bringing your assistant along?" I bit my lip, waiting for his answer.

"Sure," he said, dashing my hopes to have him for myself. "I have to have help for the type of magic I do. Lana's my right hand. I don't know how I'd function without her."

"Oh," I said. He sure knew how to say the wrong thing to me. Trying to hide my disappointment, I put on a bright expression and asked, "Do you think you'll be doing the dove illusions?"

He nodded, apparently not noticing my discomfort. "They're the mainstay of my act now. In fact, I may have a few new things up my sleeve, things I do only for kids."

"I can't wait to see."

"I'm going to be busy for the next few weeks, but we can get together a few days before the show, and I'll run through everything for you."

"Sure, that would be great," I said flatly, unable to pretend his answer was the one I wanted to hear. I didn't want to wait until the show to see him again, I wanted to see him sooner, much sooner. Like that night, if possible.

Perry glanced at the clock on the wall. "I'd better get started," he said. "Got your notebook ready?"

"Sure," I said, pulling it out of my bag.

I went to my seat feeling dejected. Even though Perry had agreed to do the show, his initial reluctance bothered me. In fact, his whole attitude toward me that day was making me uneasy. It wasn't that Perry wasn't glad to see me, just that he wasn't glad enough. Not only had he not mentioned anything about our getting together after the workshop the way he had the other day, but his remark about being busy made it clear that I wasn't supposed to expect to see him anytime in the near future. I had no idea what it was that would be tying him up for the next few weeks, but it was apparently something he had no desire to share with me. *He probably has a bunch of hot dates lined up with Lana,* I thought. He had virtually admitted that she was a big part of his life, calling her his right hand and everything. How could I ever hope to compete with someone who was not only beautiful and sexy but valuable, too?

Once Perry's lecture began, I tried to blank out all the personal stuff and concentrate on what he was talking about. Despite my newly jumbled emotions, I found him fascinating. He began his talk with a little history, explaining the types of magic performed by the Egyptians over three thousand years ago. Perry always took on a whole new attitude when he spoke about magic. His eyes fired up, and his voice became rich with excitement when describing an illusion or telling stories about some of the great magicians of the past. Just looking at him, I could tell how important magic was to his life. Yet it made me sad to realize that he might never let me get close enough to share his enthusiasm with him.

About an hour into his talk and demonstration, I noticed Perry's face darken as someone entered the room. Turning around a little, I saw a tall, broad-shouldered blond boy whose body tapered down to the narrowest hips I've seen this side of a jeans commercial. There was a swagger in his walk as he ambled over to a seat in the back. He looked to be around my age, and several times during the workshop, I found myself turning my head to get another look. He was the type of guy who practically demanded such attention, and I was curious about who he was and why he seemed to make Perry uncomfortable.

Once when I looked back, the boy's eyes met mine in a stare so intense it made me feel terribly embarrassed. Sensing a blush rise to my face, I quickly whipped around to face the front of the room and bent my head, pretending to jot down some notes on what Perry was saying. I was sure the boy was still staring at me, but I refused to turn around again. I didn't want to give him any encouragement.

At around twelve the workshop broke up, although a group of boys immediately ran up to Perry and practically attacked him with a barrage of questions. I took my time gathering my things, waiting to see how long it would take Perry to break up the session and approach me for our private lesson. But he showed no sign of doing that. No sooner did the first crowd of boys leave than Perry was deluged with a second crowd of aspiring magicians eager for advice.

I felt awkward about waiting around the room now, unwilling to stand alongside the younger boys like a puppy waiting for a treat from its master. So I got up to head for the bathroom, where I planned to freshen up and wait for the crowd to thin out. Seeing no reaction from Perry, I slowly began to make my way toward the door.

When I got there, I found that the threshold was being blocked by the boy who'd been staring at me. Now he was leaning his six-foot-plus frame across the entire width of the door. "Going somewhere?" he asked.

"Is there some special reason you should know?"

"I always make a point of finding out all I

can about beautiful girls who hang out here. What's your name?"

"Nicki. Nicki Petersen. And to whom do I have the pleasure of speaking?" I asked sarcastically, not bothering to mask my irritation.

"Hey, Nicki. Nice name." He rested a hand on his hip. "I'm Simon Kingsley. My dad runs this place."

"How nice for you," I said flatly.

"I think so." Simon held out his hand and with a few twists of the wrist produced one and then two sponge balls out of nowhere.

"Oh, so you're a magician, too," I said, then gave a bored sigh.

Simon smiled, refusing to acknowledge my not so subtle hint. "Only the best junior magician in L.A.—no matter what some people might think." He grunted in Perry's direction. "You come here for Ingram's workshop?"

I nodded. "He's really good."

Simon chuckled. "Excuse me, but by that remark I can see you don't know too much about magic. Ingram's OK on the kid stuff, but the advanced is way beyond his league. You ought to come to one of *my* workshops sometime and see a real pro at work."

Simon looked so smug it was almost nauseating. I was no expert, but I knew enough about magic to realize that his assessment of Perry's abilities was way off. I figured that the two of them must be rivals of some sort.

"But then again," he continued, "if you're really interested, I could give you a private show right now."

"Got nothing better to do with your time, huh? Well, actually, I'm waiting for Perry." I swung my head over to glance at Perry, who was still in deep conversation with the boys. "He's going to help me with a card trick."

"So where are you going then?"

"I don't have to answer that."

"Suit yourself." Simon shrugged. "Though I must admit I'm surprised. Ingram usually spends his Saturday afternoons with Lana."

"Lana?" I nearly choked on the name.

"Sure," Simon went on, noting my interest. "You must know about Lana. She and Ingram are practically inseparable around this place. Have been for years."

I didn't know who I wanted to kill first—Perry for having deceived me yet again or Simon for being the bearer of the awful news. Suddenly the room seemed ten degrees hotter, and I felt the blood rush to my cheeks. My worst fears had been confirmed; Lana and Perry were a couple. I knew there was no way I could stand up to the challenge, no way I could compete successfully with the more glamorous, more sophisticated, and, at this point, more confident Lana. What could I possibly offer Perry that she couldn't?

My only thought just then was to get back at Perry somehow, to make him pay for having led me along so cruelly. How convenient it was for me to have my weapon standing right in front of me. "Simon," I began, "I've reconsidered your offer. I would like to see your act. See, I'm coordinating a magic show for a school in the Valley, and I'm scouting around for talent. Think you might be up for it?"

"A kids' magic show? Amateur stuff," he said, brushing aside my request. But then he looked into my eyes and added, "I suppose I could use the practice, though. Sure, sign me up."

"I wouldn't want to put you out, Simon," I said sweetly. "If you feel it's below your level, I'll understand."

"Oh, no," Simon said quickly. "I think it'd be fun. Lots of fun. Besides, it would give us a chance to see more of each other, wouldn't it, Nicki?"

"Yes, I suppose it would," I said, casting one final glance at Perry. There didn't seem to be any reason to wait around for him now. "Why don't you walk me back to my car, and I'll tell you more about it?"

"Sure thing," he said, taking my hand and leading me through the hallway.

I couldn't tell if Perry got a good look at us walking out together. But I hoped he had.

Chapter Ten

The next Thursday Sara ran up to the cafeteria door where I was waiting to meet her for lunch. "Come on, Nicki," she said, practically dragging me by my elbow down the hall. "We don't have much time."

"Where are we going?"

Sara had a twinkle in her eye. "Prospecting," she said simply.

I had to run to keep up with her as she sped to her car, and I was nearly breathless by the time I fell inside. I had no idea where she was taking me, but with only a half hour to spare, it had to be someplace close. "Where to this time? Burger King? Taco Bell?" I asked, rattling off the places where a lot of kids from school hung out during lunch period.

"No, all you see there are the same old faces. Besides, I'm fed up with immature high-school boys."

"Don't tell me we're not going to eat. I'm hungry."

"Not to worry. I was sitting in Jackson's chemistry class, zoning out as usual, when inspiration struck. We're going to eat lunch near the college today."

Since the campus was a good five miles away, I didn't see how we'd have much time left for eating, let alone for serious boy-watching. But who was I to argue with Sara over the matter? She was as much entitled to fantasizing as anyone else was.

Ten minutes later we pulled up to Benny's, a local fast-food restaurant about a quarter of a mile from the state university campus.

And Sara's fantasy came face to face with coldhearted reality.

"Looks like today's not your day," I commented as soon as we stepped into the glass-walled establishment.

"I don't get it," Sara said. "Jan Geiger told me the place was always swarming with older guys."

"I guess she forgot to mention how much older they were."

As far as boys were concerned, the trip was a total waste. At the counter were a couple of middle-aged men from the nearby phone company plant, and along the wall were a few beefy guys in flannel shirts, whose buttons looked like they'd pop after their next bite of food. Assorted other men, all of whom looked old enough to be my father, were scattered around the restaurant. The two Oriental children sitting at a corner table with their mother were the only other ones there under twenty.

"I was going to get a salad, but now I guess it doesn't matter," Sara grumbled as she ordered a chili cheeseburger and fries. "We came all the way over here for nothing."

"At least the food's good," I said, trying to offer some consolation.

We paid the cashier and took our burgers to an open table in the middle of the room. "In all the magic books I've read, I've yet to come across a technique for making the check disappear," I joked, trying to get Sara's mind off her disappointment.

"Speaking of magic, how's your show coming along?" Sara asked, taking the seat with a view of the parking lot.

I bit into my burger. "I don't want to talk about it." I'd already gone four whole days without mentioning the situation with Perry, and with Sara's own heartbreak over Carl, she hadn't even noticed.

"But you were so excited about it last week. What happened? Did Chris swipe your cards or something?"

"That I could handle," I said.

"So what gives?"

I shook my head. "You're so upset about Carl I don't want to bother you with my boy problems."

"What's the magic show have to do with boys? Or is that a stupid question? C'mon, Nicki, maybe I could help."

"OK," I said, finally, feeling the need to talk. "As you know, I was hoping to get Perry involved with the show. He agreed to do it, but I haven't heard from him since I asked him on Saturday. And I'm betting now that I'll never hear from him again."

"Maybe Perry's been too busy to call," Sara mumbled through a mouthful of chili cheeseburger.

"Yeah, busy with Lana, I imagine." I sighed.

"You think she's a big part of the picture?"

"I know she is. At least that's what Simon tells me."

"Wait a sec. Let's rewind this. Who's Simon?"

"He's this guy I met at the workshop last weekend. He told me Perry and Lana have been going together for a long time."

"Maybe Perry's getting tired of her now that he's met you."

The thought of Perry with Lana ruined my appetite completely, and I put down my burger.

"I don't know, Sara. After what I did Saturday, I'm convinced he'll never call again."

"I'm almost afraid to ask. What happened this time?"

"After Simon told me the details about Perry and Lana, I got so mad I decided not to wait around for Perry as I'd planned to. I left the House of Cards with Simon, hoping that Perry would notice and get so jealous he'd come running after me. But he didn't, and now I wonder if I did the right thing."

Sara put down her soda and gave me a meaningful look. "Maybe he didn't see you, Nicki. He's probably convinced you're not interested in him now that you've stood him up a second time."

"But I didn't mean to! Or maybe part of me did. Sometimes I wonder whether I'm just driving myself crazy with him. I'd like to be with him as a real girlfriend, not as someone he could exchange for Lana whenever he felt like it. I don't like doing things halfway, and if I can't have him all for myself, I might as well forget him for good. . . . Oh, but there's the way he looks at me when we talk and the way he treated me that night at the House of Cards. I know he's really interested. But something is keeping him from admitting it. And sometimes I feel that if he's going to keep his distance from me, I've got to do the same and hold back from him. Oh, I just don't know what to do."

"What about this Simon?" Sara asked. "He's a magician, too, isn't he?"

"Please, let's not talk about Simon."

Sara leaned closer. "Now I'm definitely interested. What's your problem with him?"

"Unfortunately," I said, "I think he's interested in me."

Sara took a sip of her soda and said, "So what's the problem? Why not forget Perry and go out with him?"

"Because he's not Perry—besides which he's got a tremendous ego, and I have no desire to get involved with someone so obviously in love with himself. Only now I've stupidly got him thinking I care about him. When I was trying to get Perry jealous, I asked Simon to be in the show, too. Now he's been calling me every night, wondering when we can get together to practice. Somehow I get the feeling his idea of practice and mine are two entirely different things."

Sara lifted an eyebrow. "I don't know, Nicki. He doesn't sound so bad to me."

"You'd have to see him to understand. He's all looks and no heart. My problem now is I can't un-invite him to the show, so it looks like I've got to spend the next month dodging him."

Sara looked at her watch. "We'd better head back," she said. Then, rising, she added, "Look,

Nicki, maybe you'd better forget magicians entirely and concentrate on someone completely different. Like him," she said, pointing to one of the flannel shirts.

"More your type," I said dryly, and then we both laughed.

But suddenly just the thought of being with any guy other than Perry made me resolve to work out a solution to the mess I'd gotten myself involved in.

Chapter Eleven

Sara had been right about one thing. It would be good for me to get my mind off Perry—at least for the purpose of doing better in school. I had a math test coming up the following day, and there was no way I was going to get through it unless I shut everything else in the world out of my mind. So after dinner that night, I closed myself in my room with my math book and calculator and got down to work.

Oh, the agony. I wasn't even sure why I was taking math this year—computer math, no less—except that both my father and my counselor expected me to. I'd only been studying for ten minutes or so when I realized that I was in real trouble. I'd never had any difficulty with sums or simple calculations, but when it came to log bases and radians, I was completely lost.

It didn't help matters any that every time I

seemed close to solving a problem, the phone rang. Mom and Dad were out playing bridge, and Chris was at a friend's house, so I had to answer it. It was just as well, since all the calls were for me, anyway. First Sara phoned to tell me about the new blouses she'd picked up that afternoon, then Robin, a girl from my English class, to ask what our reading assignment was; then Caroline with the answer to a math problem I'd been grappling with; and right after I hung up with her, Sara called to complain that she still hadn't heard from Carl.

"That's enough!" I cried, ready to throw the phone out the window. I wished I had an unlisted number.

But the phone rang again two minutes later.

"L.A. International Airport," I said sarcastically.

"Uh, isn't this two-five-six, three-nine—"

"Perry?" I asked, although I already knew the answer.

"Is that you, Nicki?"

I rose from my desk and lay down on my bed. "It's been a madhouse around here tonight; the phone's been ringing continually. What's up, Perry?" My casual tone belied the tension I felt at the sound of his voice.

"This is the first chance I've had to call in days. I wanted to let you know I'm sorry I missed you after the workshop."

114

"Me, too," I admitted.

"Really?" He sounded surprised. "I didn't expect to be stopped by those guys afterward, but when I looked around for you, you'd disappeared."

So he hadn't seen me leave with Simon. "I felt funny about hanging around. I thought you'd forgotten about getting together with me," I told him.

"I'd never do that, Nicki, but I guess I should have said something earlier. You must have been mad."

"Not mad . . . just disappointed. I'd been looking forward to spending the time with you."

"If you want, we could get together early Sunday afternoon for a little while and practice."

"Really? I think I may take you up on that offer, Perry."

"We'd have to meet at the club, though. Do you mind?"

"Not at all. It's a pretty neat place." I would have met him in a dungeon if it meant a chance for the two of us to be together. I was so happy he asked, the thought of Lana didn't even enter my mind.

"Great. But the real reason I called you tonight was to ask if you'd like another magician for the show. I told my dad about it, and he'd like to help out, too."

"Your dad? That'd be terrific, Perry."

"I'm glad you think so. He's really good, and believe it or not, this would give us the opportunity to perform together for the first time."

"What kind of magic does he do?"

"I'll let him tell you all about it. He wants to talk to you, so I'll put him on now. It was nice talking to you, Nicki. I'll see you Sunday. How does twelve-thirty sound?"

"Just fine. Uh, Perry, I'm glad you called."

A split second later a booming, resonant voice came on the other end. "Nicki, I'm Harry Ingram."

"Hello, Mr. Ingram. Perry's told me what a fine magician you are."

"I've had my share of success, though my son's working hard to prove he's the best illusionist in the Ingram family. Anyway, I'd like to show you he's not the only one. I'd be happy to participate in the show you're producing."

"I'm honored, Mr. Ingram. You know I can't pay you, though."

"Consider it my gift to the children."

"Thank you, that's very nice."

"There's just one thing. As you may know, I perform with large illusions and need a fair-sized stage. That won't be a problem, will it?"

Automatically I envisioned the man trying to saw a woman in half between Mrs. Radner's desk and the blackboard and could see that it was not going to work out. Still, I had to find a way to use him in the show—for the kids' sake as well as for my standing with Perry.

"Don't worry, Mr. Ingram," I told him. "I'll take care of everything."

Chapter Twelve

Perry was waiting on the steps of the House of Cards when I arrived that Sunday afternoon. At first I thought it was another boy basking in the hot sun, but as I got closer the sight of the slim body stretched out in his T-shirt and running shorts set off a familiar feeling of anticipation.

"Working on your tan, I see," I said. I was standing right in front of him, blocking the sun.

"Oh, hi, Nicki," he said opening his eyes. The breeze gusting around us tousled his hair in a way that gave him an appealing, casual look. "I was just taking a break. Those wind sprints can tire a guy out."

"I didn't know you ran."

He pointed to his T-shirt: Canyon High School Track. "Used to be on the team but don't have time for it anymore. I still like to get out there and cover some ground, though."

"I do a little running myself," I said, sitting down on the step below him. "Did three miles this morning." I neglected to mention that I'd walked the last mile or so.

"It really clears the mind, doesn't it? I get some of my best inspiration when I run. Just now I thought of a new twist to my two-dove illusion. Say, you want to do a quick jog around the grounds? It's really pretty out back."

"I don't think so," I answered quickly. "I'm anxious to get to work on my card problems. I even brought my own deck."

He smiled. "That's like bringing an Atari to a video arcade." He started up the steps. "Let's go inside. With the winds blowing so hard, this is no place to play around with cards."

Taking my hand Perry led me into the mansion. He intertwined his fingers in mine as if forming a bond to insure that I wouldn't escape from his grasp. I liked that, although I was too nervous to offer much of a response.

We arrived at a small room on the third floor. Actually, a closet would be a better name for it. The wood-paneled space was big enough only for a round, felt-topped table, four wooden chairs, and Perry and me. "No one will disturb us in here," he said. "Now what would you like to start with?"

"I've been practicing one of the shuffles in that book you told me about," I began, "but somehow it doesn't seem right."

"Let me see," he said.

The sleight was impossible enough to do without the added pressure of wanting to impress Perry. The first time I tried it for him, I did pull it off—but it took me about ten times longer than it should have.

"You've been working on this what, a week now?" he asked. "It's not perfect, as you know, but it's pretty good for starters."

"Do you think I might be able to get this down by the time of my magic show?"

"Anything's possible. But there's another kind of shuffle you can use—the Hindu shuffle—that's a lot easier and that produces some of the same effects. It's something my grandfather showed me. Want to see?"

"Do I ever."

"Just give me the old pasteboards and let me do my stuff," he said in a slightly inaccurate imitation of W.C. Fields.

As Perry demonstrated the shuffle (which did look a lot easier), he said, "I hear you asked Simon to join your show, too." He didn't sound too thrilled.

"I met him at the workshop and happened to mention it. He jumped at the chance."

"I'll bet he did." Perry ribboned the cards on the table and then flipped them over.

I shrugged. "The more magicians the merrier. Certainly for the kids."

"Sure. And Simon's a good magician," he said, trying to brighten up his voice. He'll put on a great show."

"Yeah, that's what he said." I chuckled. "I didn't know whether to believe him or not. He seems too sure of himself."

"You can believe him. Simon happens to be one of those golden boys who can do anything he sets out to do."

I definitely detected a note of jealousy in Perry's voice, but I couldn't really understand why he'd be jealous of Simon. Perry was a much better person in so many respects. I couldn't imagine Simon taking precious time out of his schedule to teach me card tricks. In all the calls he'd made to me bragging about his talents, he had never once volunteered to help me. Lately I'd managed to avoid him simply by having my mother answer the phone and tell him I was out.

"Simon doesn't always get everything he wants," I said. "A lot of times a guy like that gets away with murder simply because no one around him bothers to give him a challenge."

"Well, there's something Simon wants very

badly—and he's not going to get it if I have anything to do about it."

Was Perry referring to me? "Are you and Simon after the same thing?" I asked, catching my breath.

"Yes," Perry said without elaborating. He picked up the deck and shuffled it loosely a few times. "Let's get back to the cards. Here's an effect you can do using that shuffle. It's a good one to perform for children, too."

Perry demonstrated a few times, and that seemed to relax him. Then he handed me the cards and asked me to repeat his moves. I had a little trouble; my fingers kept getting caught up in the cards. Grinning good-naturedly, Perry clasped his hands over mine and guided me through the maneuver. His touch was secure yet surprisingly gentle. I wished my hands hadn't been holding the cards because at that moment more than anything else I wanted to clasp Perry's hands, to release some of the pent-up feelings for him that were simmering inside me.

I sensed something going on inside Perry, too. He seemed to hold my hands a bit longer than necessary to just show me the shuffle. I also felt a slight tremor in his fingers. Slowly his hands began to slide up my arms. The movement was so unexpected yet so welcome I shivered involuntarily and let the cards fall to the table.

It was just like that night in the close-up room. That gesture, as slight as it was, was enough to shatter the mood for Perry. He withdrew his hands, returning them to the table.

"I'm sorry, Nicki," he said.

My heart cried out, *What are you sorry for?* but my mouth remained silent. I didn't have the courage then to ask Perry why he felt the need to hold back. I was afraid to hear his answer.

From then on Perry was all business. We must have spent more than two hours in that little room, I showing Perry what little I knew, he giving me plenty of encouragement and tips on improvement, although now without the added inducement of touch. He did volunteer a few bits of information about himself, like how he had started a magic club at his school and how he first got involved in illusions by trying to make the rocks in his rock collection disappear. But these tidbits came only between tricks. When he had the cards in his hands, it was as if they made up his entire universe.

I think we both would have been content to stay in that room for the entire day. But our pleasant solitude was shattered by a harsh knock on the door. The intruder didn't bother to wait for us to say "Come in" before she did just that.

It was Lana, looking as beautiful as ever in a short sweat-shirt dress. "Perry, so this is where you've been hiding." Her hands moved to her hips as she glared down impatiently at him. I felt invisible. "They told me you were around here somewhere. Do you realize it's nearly three o'clock?"

"It is?" Perry rose in a panic. "Oh, Nicki, excuse me. I—I've got to go," he blabbered. "Uh, Lana, I'd like you to meet Nicki. Nicki, Lana." He was at the door, leaving me sitting alone and bewildered against the back wall. "I'll call you soon, OK?"

"Sure." What else could I say?

And with that he was gone.

I remained in the little room for a few more minutes. Everything had been so perfect until *she* came. Why did she have to spoil everything? And why did Perry go running after her as if he were her personal slave?

I knew I wouldn't be getting any immediate answers. But I felt as if I had to do something. So, taking the cards in my hands, I neatened them into a tight little pile, then picked them up and hurled them against the wall.

Chapter Thirteen

The only thing that kept me going over the next two days was Perry's promise that he'd call me. Despite my earlier resolve, I came to realize my infatuation for him now ran so deep I couldn't simply blank him out of my mind. If I had to share him with Lana for now, so be it. Someday I'd manage to win him over to my side for good. For the first time ever, I was willing to fight for a boy I wanted.

In any event, I could still look forward to seeing him at my magic show. On Tuesday afternoon I had to ask Mrs. Radner to help me get permission to move the show into the school auditorium. Of course if we did that, it would no longer be the simple treat she had envisioned for her students alone, and I hoped that that would be OK with her.

"Good news, Mrs. Radner," I said as I

walked into the reading center. "The magic show is really mushrooming into something big."

"Not too big, I hope," she said. "As you can see, this room isn't very large."

"That's what I want to talk to you about. I think it *has* gotten too big for the reading center. Uh, do you think we can use the school's auditorium instead?"

"Why the auditorium?" she asked.

I proceeded to tell her how I'd gotten a whole bunch of performers, including a world-famous magician, to work for free. Referring to Mr. Ingram, I said, "He's performed for royalty and presidents and in the finest arenas all over the world." I knew I was stretching the truth since I was only guessing as to where Mr. Ingram had put on his act, but it was important that Mrs. Radner be impressed. "Now, he's consented to come to this school to introduce these children to the wonders of magic. You can't expect him to be comfortable doing that squeezed in between desks, can you?"

"No, of course not," Mrs. Radner said. "But, Nicki, this was supposed to be a special treat just for these children."

"It's more of a treat now than ever—a genuine magic show with a real professional magician. And I don't think the kids will mind opening up the show to the rest of the school, do you? Why should they? It'll certainly be better this way than having no show at all."

"You're right, Nicki," Mrs. Radner said after a momentary pause. "There's not that much time, but I'll see what I can arrange with the principal."

"It's going to be the best thing this school's seen in years," I boasted confidently. "Just you wait and see, Mrs. Radner, you're not going to be disappointed."

With that I sauntered off to Mitchell and Mary Beth. As usual Mitchell was at his machine, reading away almost effortlessly about jungle life in Brazil. Mary Beth, on the other hand, was sitting restlessly in her seat. Her machine was turned on, but she looked as if she'd rather be anywhere else in the world.

"What are you going to read for me today, Mary Beth?" I asked.

She smiled impishly. "It all depends," she said.

"Depends on what?"

"On whether you'll do another trick for me today."

"Hmm, I smell blackmail here," I said. "No tricks today."

"Just one?" she asked.

"No," I said. You had to be firm with kids or else they were liable to walk all over you. For a would-be teacher that's suicide.

"C'mon, Nicki, just one teensy trick. That's all. Please?"

Uh-oh. She had one of Chris's doe-eyed looks on her face, and since she was a lot younger and more innocent looking, it really tugged at my heartstrings. *It wouldn't be so bad to do just one short trick for her, would it? Yes,* my better judgment answered. Mary Beth was here at the reading center to learn how to read better, and she wouldn't do that if her time was taken up with magic tricks. If I let her coax me into doing one, how much more persuasion would it take to make me do another and another and another?

But maybe there was a way to compromise. "I tell you what, Mary Beth. For every story you read to me, I'll do a trick for you," I said.

"Great," she answered. "Let me see one."

"No, you've got to read to me first."

"How do I know you'll do the trick?"

"I'll put it down in writing. How's that?" I said, reaching for one of my notebooks. Ripping out a sheet of paper, I printed carefully: *I, Nicki Petersen, will perform a magic trick after Mary Beth Segovia reads one story.* After I signed my name, I handed the sheet to the little girl. "Does this meet with your approval?"

Silently Mary Beth mouthed the words on the paper. She read at an excruciatingly slow pace. "Deal," she said finally.

We shook hands, and she proceeded to go through her reading lesson. I was afraid it would be nighttime by the time she got through, but she finished in less than fifteen minutes.

"Now it's your turn," she said, looking quite pleased with herself.

"You deserve a special magic trick. You did very well today," I said.

I reached into my purse and took out the deck of cards I always carried with me. This was as good a time as any to practice one of the new tricks I was working on. Sorting through the pile, I pulled out a card and asked Mary Beth to name it.

"The ace of spades," she said.

"Good," I said, putting it down. Then I cut the deck in half and began a Faro shuffle so that one half of the deck stuck out from the top of the other half. I held the top half away from me so that the cards faced Mary Beth. "Say 'stop' when you see a card you like," I explained as I flicked the cards forward slowly.

"Stop!" she cried solemnly. She was taking this very seriously.

"OK, now remember that card," I said. Then I turned the top part of the deck so that it was at a right angle to the rest of the cards. "Do you know what I have here?" I asked. "A card gun. And remember this ace of spades?" I picked it up from the table. "This is the bullet. I'm going to load the ace into the bottom of the gun," I said as I slipped it into the deck, "and it's going to fire the card you picked a minute ago right at you." Taking aim, I "fired" the "gun" in Mary Beth's direction, and a card landed face down on her desk.

"What was your card?" I asked her.

"The seven of hearts," she answered.

"Now turn that card over," I commanded. She did, and, sure enough, there was the seven of hearts.

"How'd you do that?" she demanded excitedly.

"Just lucky, I guess."

"Let me see another," she pleaded.

"No, we made a deal. One trick for each story read. Now it's getting late, and I've got to go. I'll see you next week."

"If I read more, will you do more tricks for me?" she asked.

"That's all up to you, Mary Beth. You keep your part of the deal, and I'll keep mine." I wasn't sure whether I was using good teaching strategy or not, but as long as it got her to read, I didn't see anything wrong with it.

Two nights later I called the Ingram house. Mr. Ingram answered on the first ring. "Well, hello, Nicki," he said. "Do you want to speak to Perry?"

"Yes," I said, "but my main reason for calling was to speak to you. I wanted to let you know the arrangements for the show are all set now. I don't think you'll have any problems."

"Good work, young lady. We'll put on a show they'll remember for years to come."

"Funny, that's what I told the teacher. It ought to be super. Can you put Perry on, Mr. Ingram? I'd like to tell him, too."

"Sorry, Nicki, but he's at the club right now. That boy is at the House of Cards so much, sometimes I think we ought to ship his bed over there. Listen, Nicki, I have an idea. Why don't you join us for dinner this Saturday, and we can discuss all the details together then?"

How could I say no to a chance to see Perry again? "I'd be happy to come," I said. "I can't think of a better way to spend this Saturday night."

Chapter Fourteen

"Will you cut it out? You look great." Sara was standing behind me at my bathroom vanity, putting the finishing touches on my hair. She'd spent over an hour giving me a new look, parting my hair on the side instead of letting it hang from the middle, and combing it straight back over my ears. It was different all right, and I wasn't sure I liked it.

"What do you think, Caroline?" I asked. At times like this a second opinion from an unbiased source was desperately needed.

Caroline looked up from her history book as she perched on the bathtub rim. "Sara's right, you look fine and have nothing to worry about. Unlike me."

"What's the matter, Caroline, having trouble with the Civil War?" I asked.

"No, that's a snap. It's the French Revolution I'm hung up on."

"Why are you bothering with that? You're not taking European history this year."

"No, but I've got to know it for the decathlon. That was my downfall at the last meet," she said. "I'm supposed to be the history expert, but I keep forgetting which side Robespierre was on."

"Maximilien de Robespierre was the leader during France's Reign of Terror. He was quite revolutionary," Sara said, putting down my comb.

Caroline and I looked at her in amazement. "I thought everyone knew that," Sara said innocently. Then, pointing at my face in the mirror, she added, "Now tell me I'm not the world's greatest stylist and French history expert."

"You're not the world's greatest stylist and French history expert," Caroline and I said in unison.

"Come on, Caroline," Sara insisted, taking hold of my cheeks. "Isn't this the face that's going to bowl over the Ingram family tonight?"

"I still don't know why you're going to all this trouble," Caroline said. "It's only dinner."

"Tonight dinner, tomorrow who knows?" I said, turning my head from side to side inspecting my new look. A week had passed since Perry had last seen me, and I wanted to make a lasting impression on him that night.

"Just don't be *too* nice to Perry's mom and dad," Sara warned. "Boys can tell pretty easily when a girl's trying to get to them through their parents—and they don't like it."

"That's not my style, Sara," I said, sauntering back to my room. As the girls followed me inside, I continued, "Perry's father invited me. I didn't invite myself. He sounded like an interesting person over the phone, and whatever conversations I have with him will take place because I want to talk to him, not because I'm trying to score points with Perry." I opened up my closet door and pulled out my lavender V-necked dress.

"Is that what you're wearing?" Sara asked.

"Yeah, what's wrong with it?"

"Oh, nothing," she said. "It just looks a little dressy to wear over to somebody's house. I thought you'd go in a nice pants outfit or something."

Shaking my head I said, "I figure if things go well, Perry might want to take me to the House of Cards tonight, and I can't get in there without a dress."

A few hours later I was standing on the front steps of the Ingrams' house. They lived in a fancy area off Laurel Canyon called Mount Olympus, which had a lot of crazily curved streets with names like Electra and Jupiter and

Apollo. Even though Perry's father had been meticulous with his directions, I made a couple of wrong turns and ended up going around in what appeared to be a big circle until I found the turnoff into Perry's street.

I parked right in front of the white stucco house and walked up to the door, where a short, well-tailored woman with Perry's dark hair and features answered my ring. "Mrs. Ingram? Hi, I'm Nicki Petersen."

The woman's face lit up in a smile. "Welcome, Nicki, it's a pleasure to meet you at last."

I wasn't sure what the "at last" was about, but as I stepped into the tiled foyer, I handed her the box of candy I'd brought for her.

"Thank you," she said, leading me into the living room. Seated on one of the Haitian cotton sofas was a distinguished-looking man with a thick shock of white hair. "Nicki, I'd like you to meet Mr. Ingram."

The old man started to rise. "You don't have to get up for me, sir," I said, immediately taking a seat next to him on the sofa.

"That's very kind of you, Nicki," he said. "At my age these old bones don't jump up as easily as they once did."

I was more than a little shocked. I had no idea Perry's father was so old. His voice sounded different from the booming one on the phone, too, and I couldn't help but wonder how he would manage to work his way through an entire magic act. "I bet you forget all about that when you're performing," I told him.

"Oh, no, dear, I'm afraid I haven't put on a show in a dog's age. Oh, every now and again I'll do a few tricks at the club or help Perry out with a thing or two, but I just don't have the stamina of the old days."

The old days? "Uh, aren't you Perry's father?"

"Nicki," Mrs. Ingram interrupted, "this is Perry's *grand*father."

I felt a blush creep up my cheeks, but the older Mr. Ingram patted my leg and chuckled. "You just made my day, Nicki. That was the nicest compliment I've been given in a long time."

"I should have been more specific with my introduction," Mrs. Ingram said. "Actually we know him better around here as Pops."

"Which I'd like you to call me, too," Mr. Ingram said.

"OK, Pops," I said, feeling a little awkward about getting on such familiar terms so quickly. "By the way, where's Perry?"

"He ought to be along any minute now," Mrs. Ingram said. "He's been practicing at the club all day." She rose, straightening the lines of her attractive blue knit dress. "I'd better check on dinner. The weather's so nice we decided to make a barbecue tonight. The other Mr. Ingram's out back now, starting up the grill. He should be coming inside any minute now."

"Is there anything I can do to help?" I asked.

"No, everything's under control. Why don't you wait right here for Perry in the meantime."

I wanted to ask her why Perry wasn't already here if he knew I was coming, but I kept my mouth shut. Turning back to Pops, I said, "You must be really proud of your grandson."

"As proud as the day is long." The old man's eyes crinkled as he spoke. "The boy's come a long way. He's going to be a great one, I think. Naturally, I'm prejudiced."

"He's spoken very highly of you, too. The first time I met Perry he showed me an effect you had taught him. He says you've been a great inspiration to him."

"There's nothing that pleases a magician more than being able to hand down his craft to the next generation. And it's a joy to see a boy like Perry take what I give him and mold it to his own personality." He sighed. "Reminds me of my own performing days."

"What were they like?" I asked eagerly.

Pops leaned back against his pillow and turned his gaze upward as he collected his thoughts. "When I first started out, we still had vaudeville. Let me tell you, it was a tough grind doing show after show, night after night, criss-crossing back and forth across the country, sometimes not knowing what city we'd be performing in next. One night we'd work the old Fox Theatre in Saint Louis, for instance, and the next night we'd be stuck in some rickety old auditorium in the middle of a cornfield. Ah, but what wonderful times they were. Picked up some of my best illusions in those small towns. Then, later on I got to work with some of the finest. Like Blackstone—I named my son after him you know. And there was also Leipzig and Dante, among others—"

"Pops, I see you're already boring Nicki with your old stories."

I looked up at a man with black hair that was graying at the temples and with the same chiseled jawline as Perry's. "Hi, Nicki, I'm Harry Ingram. I see you've already met my father."

"Yes, and he's fascinating," I said, rising to shake the man's hand.

"Dinner's almost ready. I don't know where that son of mine is, but we may just have to eat without him."

"Maybe we could wait a little while longer?" The thought of starting without Perry was making me lose my appetite.

"Pops, did Nicki tell you she's a magician, too?"

"No, she didn't," Mr. Ingram said. "But I already knew that. Perry filled me in."

"I'm nowhere near Perry's caliber, though,"

I told him. "Not yet. I just like to fool around with cards for my own pleasure."

"Nothing wrong with that," Pops said and smiled. "Every magician worth his salt starts out by simply trying to entertain himself. Or herself. Weren't any girl magicians back in my day, but I'm glad to see that that's changed."

Just then the phone rang, and Perry's father picked it up. His face fell as he listened. Putting down the receiver, he said, "Nicki, I've got some bad news. Perry's not going to be able to make it. He's staying at the club to catch an act he's been waiting months to see. I'm sorry."

"I—I don't know what to say." I felt as if I should leave. The Ingrams were being very friendly to me, but without Perry, there didn't seem to be any real reason for my presence.

"Of course you'll still stay and have dinner with us," Mr. Ingram said. "I insist."

What could I do? So the four of us sat down to a dinner of steaks and potatoes. At first Perry's father wanted to hear the latest news of our magic show. He went on to tell me how much he welcomed the chance to perform for children. It was a change of pace from his usual audience. He spent most of his time hopscotching between nightclub shows in Las Vegas and trade conventions around Los Angeles. Frankly, it didn't sound as exciting to me as barnstorming through the backwaters of America fifty years

139

ago, but Mr. Ingram spoke with as much enthusiasm for his craft as did his father.

After he finished the room grew quiet; it was as if Perry's absence had cast a spell over all of us. I knew why I was affected; all my planning, the hours of working on my hair, my fantasies about how Perry would see me as a girl he'd want to date—all that was gone now, and the consolation of this pleasant dinner with these near strangers wasn't enough to make up for the loss.

Then Perry's father spoke up. "Nicki, before you go off thinking that Perry is some kind of heel for not being here, I ought to tell you this: he didn't know beforehand that you were coming tonight."

I nearly dropped my fork. "Then why am I here?" I burst out. "I mean, I—I could have told you everything you needed to know about the magic show over the phone."

"I know, but I wanted to meet you in person before the show. And," he added, "I wanted a firsthand look at the girl Perry talks about all the time."

"Perry talks about me?" I said stupidly.

"You sound surprised. I'm sure you know he's very fond of you."

"I *am* surprised, Mr. Ingram. The truth of the matter is I thought he thought of me as just another magician." I figured I might as well lay all my cards on the table, so to speak.

"I imagine he hasn't had much time to spend with you, with the big show coming up. He's been terribly preoccupied with it, as you know."

"The show? But it's just a little thing for kids. He told me himself he had all kinds of tricks already prepared for it."

"I don't mean your show, Nicki—not that it's unimportant to him. I mean the House of Cards' annual membership dinner. Didn't he tell you about that?"

I was confused now. "No, he never said a word."

"That's my son," Mrs. Ingram put in. "Always modest about his own talents. I imagine he didn't tell you he was up for an award, either."

Another surprise. "No, he didn't. What kind of award?"

"Outstanding Junior Magician," she answered proudly. "And he's going to win too."

Suddenly things started to make sense. "I don't suppose Simon Kingsley is in the running for this award, too, is he?"

"Simon?" Mr. Ingram stroked his chin. "Yes. As a matter of fact, he's Perry's biggest rival. Has been ever since I first brought Perry to the club when he was— Jean, how old was Perry then?"

"Nine," Mrs. Ingram answered. "He would have gone sooner," she added, speaking to me, "but I was hoping he'd get it out of his system. Even though I married into a magician's family, I wanted to spare my son the kind of heartbreak that goes hand in hand with the craft. So very few can make a living from it these days. But Perry inherited the Ingram love of magic, and trying to take it away from him now would be like taking away a part of his soul. It means more to him than anything."

"Indeed," said Mr. Ingram. "When he started spending all his allowance money on magic gear, I saw he had the drive he'd need to go all the way to the top if he wanted, so I decided to give him all the encouragement I could."

"That's when he started going to the club?" I asked.

Mrs. Ingram excused herself and got up from the table. "I'll be right back," she said. A few moments later she returned with a scrapbook. "I thought you might like to see some photos of Perry's first performances." With the kind of pride only a mother has, she laid the book out on the table and flipped to a page near the beginning.

If the photo album had been of anyone else, I might have been embarrassed by this display, but I had to admit that I was curious to know as much about Perry as I could, especially now

142

that I realized there was so much I hadn't been aware of. From what his parents had told me so far, I got the impression I already meant more to him than he had ever let on.

"Look at this, Nicki." Mrs. Ingram pointed to a shorter, slightly pudgy-looking young Perry dressed in a black cape and wearing a painted-on black mustache. "This is Perry at nine when he put on his first show in the neighborhood."

"How cute," I said. "I like the mustache. Oh, and look at him with that top hat." I pointed to another photo obviously taken during the same show.

"Borrowed from me," Perry's father said. "As you can tell from the fit."

Mrs. Ingram flipped the page. "And here he is at his first show at the club. He was ten then."

"Who's the girl next to him?" I asked.

"That's Lana Feliciano. She's been Perry's assistant ever since that show. Such a sweet girl . . ."

That was all I needed to hear: one more voice to remind me that I was in competition with a tradition. "They must be really close," I grumbled, uncontrollably overwhelmed with jealousy for my rival.

"Not in the way you might think, Nicki," Mr. Ingram said, looking at me kindly. "With the kind of illusions Perry does, he needs an assistant. Lana's father is on the club's board of directors, and he volunteered his daughter way back when Perry was first starting out. At the time she loved the idea of getting up on stage. Perry wasn't too thrilled with the idea of performing with her back then. I remember him kicking and screaming, saying he didn't want a girl messing up his act. But they've worked very well together over the years."

"Poor Lana's getting a bit tired of it, though," Mrs. Ingram said, picking up the story. "She's not as devoted to magic as Perry is, though she's still willing to help him out until he can find someone else. From what he's told me, some of her boyfriends are upset at the amount of time she spends on it."

Boyfriends? Lana's boyfriends? The Ingrams showed me a few more snapshots, but I hardly paid attention as I attempted to absorb this new information. If Lana and Perry meant nothing to each other romantically, that meant there was real hope for me after all!

". . . and now he won't even let his father help him with his act," Mrs. Ingram was saying as I rejoined their conversation. "We won't even know what he's going to be doing until the night of the dinner."

"When is that?" I asked.

"Next weekend."

"I'm sure he's going to do just fine," I told

them. "I saw him perform a couple of weeks ago, and he blew the audience away. He was quite professional."

"I only wish he'd remember he's still only sixteen. Maybe after the dinner he'll ease up a little," Mrs. Ingram said. "One of these days he's going to have to discover there's more to life than magic wands and silk handkerchiefs."

I had the feeling she was referring in some way to me. By the time I left the Ingrams', I was convinced that I still had a chance with Perry—that is, if any girl had a chance with him. But I was also convinced that my real rival was something more potent than another girl. It remained to be seen if ordinary Nicki Petersen could compete with the strong passion Perry had for his magic.

The following Wednesday a letter came for me in the mail. The cream-colored envelope bore only the letters HOC as a return address. Quickly ripping apart the envelope, I uncovered a fancy engraved invitation asking me to attend the forty-third Annual House of Cards Membership Dinner and Awards Presentations at the Century Plaza Hotel. There was no written message to me, nothing to indicate who had sent the invitation. Obviously, it was the Ingram family who'd sent it, I reasoned, since we had talked about the affair just the other night at dinner.

It was also possible that Perry had sent the invitation, but since I hadn't heard from him in a while and I knew that he was preoccupied with the show, that didn't make sense.

In any event, I wasn't prepared for the call I got that night. "Hey, Nicki, it's me." Even over the phone I could sense the smugness. Only a boy like Simon would presume I'd remember the sound of his voice after a two-week absence.

Yet remember it I did. "Hi, Simon," I said coolly. "I imagine you got my note about the magic show. A week from Friday at two-thirty in the afternoon. You'll be there, won't you?"

"Me, give up a chance to see you again? I wouldn't miss it for anything," he said.

"Good," I said, trying to keep my tone casual. "Then I'll see you at the show."

"Hey, not so fast. I didn't call you about that. I called about the awards dinner. Did you get my invitation?"

I nearly dropped the phone. "*You* sent me that invitation?"

"Who else, Nicki? You really didn't expect one from that wimp Ingram, did you?"

"Well . . ." I began.

"He's got enough to handle with his doves. But you're going to come and root me on, aren't you? I'm up for Junior Magician of the Year, you know."

"Yes, I know," I said. "But I don't think I can accept your invitation."

"Nicki, this is the most important event of the year. Anybody who's anybody in magic's going to be there. How could you skip it?"

"I'd love to go, Simon. But in all honesty I'd feel funny being there because of you."

"Don't you want to see me win?"

"Don't make me say it, Simon."

"It's Ingram, isn't it?"

"You lied to me about him and Lana—they're just friends. He likes me, Simon, and if I went to the show, I'd be there to support him. But I'm not the kind of girl who'd do that by taking advantage of you. It wouldn't be right."

"That's very noble of you, Nicki, but I still want you to come."

"Even after what I just told you?"

"Call me stubborn. I figure once you see Ingram and me together, you may want to reconsider your decision."

"I wouldn't count on it, Simon."

"You'll be there, though?"

Under those conditions, how could I say no?

Chapter Fifteen

It seemed appropriate that the awards dinner was being held in Century City. Even though it was still early evening, the lights of the high-rise complex rose magically out of the much lower horizon surrounding it, sparkling in the night sky like an ethereal wonderland.

Dad dropped me off right in front of the Century Plaza Hotel. I'd planned on driving down myself, but the dinner was going to be a late-night affair, and my mom and dad didn't like the idea of my driving the freeways alone that far into the night. Reluctantly I agreed to let Dad take me, glad he was letting me go at all. "Call me up as soon as you have an idea when the show will be over, and I'll come get you," Dad said as he reached over to open my door.

"Will do," I answered, carefully stepping out onto the curb. Since I didn't have any fancy evening dresses to my name, Mom had loaned me one of her long narrow skirts, which, with my frilly pink blouse, would pass as acceptable attire. Once again I had crammed my feet into a pair of heels, but I'd taken the precaution of wearing them around the house for several days beforehand, trying to stretch them into a more comfortable fit. I wasn't going to let anything ruin this night for me.

After Dad left I followed the crowd into the cavernous lobby of the Century Plaza. I took the elevator down two floors to the California Level, then walked down the wide, carpeted corridor leading to the Los Angeles Room, where the dinner was being held. Taking my place in the line waiting to go inside, I found myself surrounded by glamorous-looking men in dinner jackets and women in evening gowns, silk pajamas, and ladies' tuxedos. Almost everyone was older than I, but here and there I spotted some kids my age, as well as some little kids, who darted in and out of the line. My sense of anticipation increased with every step closer to the entrance. Eavesdropping on the people surrounding me, I heard talk of nothing but magic, and I felt as if I were about to enter a private community open only to a privileged few.

Finally I handed my invitation to the boy at the door. Once inside the vast room, however, I was unsure about where to turn first. On my right was a long bar that was already crowded with people. To my left was a wall filled with photos of magicians in performance. In between were several hundred people, all beginning to congregate in small groups. There was still some time before the dining area was to be opened for seating, so I decided to head toward the photo wall.

On my way over I stopped and gasped. Standing just two feet away was Doug Henning, the real Doug Henning, chatting animatedly with a man I recognized as a TV actor. I'd seen Henning perform a couple of years earlier in Detroit, and he had seemed so much larger than life doing those incredible illusions on stage. I couldn't believe that now I was so close to him that I could actually run up and touch him if I wanted. He was a real, regular person. It would be something to get to talk to him for a while. But being cowardly, I just walked by him and smiled, and he, not seeing me, continued on with his conversation.

On the way over to the photo wall, I felt someone tap my shoulder. Had Doug noticed me after all?

No such luck.

"Hi, Nicki, glad you could make it," the voice said.

I turned around. Dressed in a powder blue tux that matched the color of his eyes, he looked even more dazzling than I'd remembered. If stage presence was all that was required, he'd win the award with no problem. "Hi, Simon," I said. "This is some crowd."

"I told you everybody was going to be here," he said. "Look over there!" Like an excited little boy, he pointed toward the middle of the room.

Peering to my right I spotted another familiar face. "That's David Copperfield!" I exclaimed. "Wow, and you're going to perform in front of him? I'd die if I had to do that."

Simon didn't say anything at first, but the look on his face as he continued to gaze at the famous magician indicated a vulnerability I didn't think possible in him. Finally he turned to me, the smug look back on his face. "Nothing to it," he said a bit too easily. "I've got my routine down backward and forward." He chuckled. "I have to 'cause it sure would be embarrassing to make a mistake in front of this crowd."

"I can't imagine you being anything but perfect," I said truthfully.

"I've got to be, Nicki. I can't let all my practicing go for nothing, can I?"

"This award means a lot to you, doesn't it?"

"You bet. It carries a lot more prestige than you might think. The guy who won two years ago is now touring the country, and last year's winner has been on TV. I've worked hard to get this far, and all I can say is Ingram better not get in the way of my glory."

"What if neither one of you wins?"

"No one else in the running is even close," he said.

I held out my hand. "Good luck, Simon. May the best boy win."

I'm glad he didn't press me to give my opinion on who the best boy was. "Thanks, I appreciate that," he said. "Look, I'm on first, and I've got to get backstage now. See you later."

The doors to the dining area had just been opened, and people were starting to filter inside. I decided to head on in when I spotted the Ingrams in front of me. "Mrs. Ingram," I called out.

She stopped at the sound of her name. "Nicki," she said when I'd gotten within several people of her. "What a pleasant surprise to see you again."

"You'll come sit with us, won't you?" asked Mr. Ingram. "Or do you have other plans?"

"No, I'd love to join you," I said. "I was hoping I could."

"It'd be my pleasure to escort such a lovely lady to her seat," said Pops, who'd taken hold of my arm.

"Where's Perry?" I asked.

"Backstage, getting ready to knock 'em dead," his father answered as we headed to a table near the front of the room. The first few rows of tables were roped off, reserved for David Copperfield and the other magic superstars and celebrities in attendance.

"I'll bet he must be pretty nervous," I said.

"I'm sure he is. The toughest audience of all is other magicians. Anyone who wasn't suffering an attack of the butterflies at this moment would be a fool."

The four of us sat down at the big, round table, where we were soon joined by four other people. One of the men introduced himself as a magician, and Pops immediately remembered him from his days on the road. He was there with his wife. The other couple—Bob and Nancy Green, we discovered as introductions were made all around—were businesspeople who used the club as a place to entertain clients.

At each place setting was a program for the evening. I picked mine up and hurriedly scanned past the menu and the list of the club's board of directors to the list of performers. As Simon had told me, he was first, following a brief introduction by the master of ceremonies. Perry would be performing right before the major awards were to be given out. My heart jumped when I saw his name. I wanted to be with him so much at that moment, to cheer for him and let him know that no matter how things went, he was still the best to me. But I knew that that was impossible. Barging in on him at this point would be the last thing he needed. Even if he was glad to see me, my unexpected arrival might throw off his concentration. And if for some reason he wasn't glad to see me . . . well, that was a possibility I wasn't even willing to entertain.

The businessman, sitting to my left, spoke up when he noticed I'd put my program down. "Are you here with the Ingrams?" he asked.

"Sort of," I said. "I came to watch their son perform tonight."

"Those pros are really something, aren't they?" he commented. "In fact, I was at the club the other day when one of the old-timers showed me something impossible." Mr. Green reached into his coat pocket and took out a handful of cards while his wife rolled her eyes as if she'd seen this bit one too many times. "He counted out these cards like this: one, two, three, four, five, six, and then threw three cards away . . ."

The old Six-Card stab. I tried to keep from smiling as he began again to count out six more cards. He had the trick down pat—I had to give him credit for that—but on the other hand he didn't know who he was dealing with.

"I'm impressed," I said when he'd finished the trick. "Could I see your cards? I have to make sure you weren't using a trick deck or anything."

"Sure." He handed over the packet.

Nonchalantly I took them in my hands and slowly shuffled. Then I spread the cards out on the table between our place settings. "I saw someone do this once, and I can't figure it out. Why don't you pick a card, but don't tell me what it is."

The man looked at me curiously but selected a card from near the center of the deck. I directed him to put it back near the center. Then I took the cards and did a few false shuffles, which I hoped looked convincing enough. Laying out the cards face up, I said, "I didn't see your card, but two of these cards here are going to help me find yours." Pretending to concentrate, I studied the cards and pulled out a four of hearts and three of spades. "I believe you picked the four of spades," I announced.

Mr. Green's mouth opened in wonder. "Don't say anything yet," I said, picking up the cards and doing another shuffle. Handing him the deck I added, "Add up the value of those two cards, count out that many cards from the top of the deck, and your card will be there."

By this time everyone at the table was watching as Mr. Green counted out seven cards. "Well, I'll be," he said, putting down the cards after he turned over the four of spades. "And I thought you were just a sweet little girl."

To my surprise the rest of the table gave me a hand. Mr. Ingram looked at me and winked. "I've seen some pros do that one, and you handled it just as smoothly as the best of them."

"Thanks," I said. It was a nice feeling being in the spotlight at a gathering like that, even playing to an audience of seven.

The next major attraction of the evening was not a magician, but a full-course meal. When the waiters arrived with the first course, I handed the cards back to Mr. Green and picked up my knife and fork.

Chapter Sixteen

Shortly after we had finished the steak dinner and the chocolate mousse, the lights dimmed, and a spotlight was focused on the stage. As I thought of Perry I felt so nervous you would have thought *I* was going to perform.

Out stepped a man I recognized as the actor who played a judge on a well-known soap opera. He was the master of ceremonies, and after reciting a few old jokes and pointing out the celebrities in attendance, he introduced the first act.

"Ladies and gentlemen, we at the House of Cards realize the future of magic lies with the younger generation. That's why we established our junior magicians workshops soon after the club was founded. Over the years our youngsters have gone on to attain success in cities all over the world. Tonight, along with our other

157

acts, we'll be featuring some of the best and brightest rising stars, all of whom are competing for the award for Junior Magician of the Year. Right now I'm pleased to present a young man who performed his first illusion when he was three—and I still can't figure out how he did it. Please give a warm hand to Simon Kingsley."

The stage went black, and seconds later, rising out of a puff of smoke, was Simon, basking in the sound of applause that rose like a wave and filled the ballroom. In his hand he carried an umbrella, which before my disbelieving eyes turned into a bouquet of flowers and back to an umbrella before Simon made the whole thing disappear into a dazzling column of red-hot fire.

This was impressive enough, but Simon was far from finished. From a platform on his right, he picked up a set of eight large rings, about ten inches in diameter, and after giving a short history of the rings and a demonstration proving they were solid, he went into a lengthy routine during which he linked and then unlinked them in an amazing manner.

I'll say this much for him: Simon's handling of the rings was as smooth as his talk. If I didn't know better, I could have sworn he was making the rings cut through each other by the sheer force of his will. The gasps that came from parts of the audience when he unveiled his finale—all eight rings united as one—told me that I wasn't the only one taken in by his illusion.

Simon left the stage to thunderous applause and headed toward the tables, where I presumed he would await the handing out of the awards. As he made his way up the aisle, he seemed to be looking for someone, and I realized who the someone was when he made eye contact with me. At first his eyes lit up, but when he saw who I was sitting with, his expression turned glum, and he quickly turned and hurried across the room to take a seat with some people who might have been his parents.

A comedy magician who was vying for the overall Magician of the Year Award appeared next, but I could hardly pay attention to him. I was thinking of Perry and what must have been going through his mind at that moment. Simon had been good, much better than I'd imagined he would be, and for the first time I began to worry that he might beat out Perry after all. Was Perry having these thoughts, too? I could tell that the Ingram family was concerned from the silence that came from their side of the table after Simon's performance.

"When does your boy go on?" the old magician asked Perry's father after the fifth act was over.

"After this next group," he said nervously. I could see he was holding Mrs. Ingram's hand very tightly.

"Don't worry, Mr. Ingram. Perry's going to do just fine," I said.

"Of course he is," echoed Mrs. Ingram.

None of us could wait for the next act to be over. It was a team that combined illusionary skills with acrobatic stunts. Under normal circumstances I would have been blown away by their act, but these were anything but normal circumstances.

Finally the soap opera judge came out again. "And now the last of our talented junior magicians. Like many who have gone through our program, he comes from a fine family of illusionists. Ladies and gentlemen, let's hear it for Perry Ingram!"

To the strains of a romantic piece of classical music, Perry walked out to center stage, looking handsome and professional in his black tuxedo. He started off by revealing a long black wand, which he promptly changed into a handkerchief and then into a dove. At that moment Lana came out wheeling a box and a stand on which she placed the bird. Perry took the box from her and held open its top for the audience to see. It was empty. After spinning the box several times, he reopened the lid and pulled out a long stream of colorful silks, which he handed to Lana. Then he showed us the top of the box, which again appeared empty. Another few spins and this time he began to extract dove after dove. The birds were supposed to fly to the stand, but one of them developed a bad case of stage fright and hovered over the ballroom for the longest time, finally resting atop the massive crystal chandelier over the center of the room.

Perry stopped short, and everyone in the room seemed to hold his breath waiting to see how he would handle the mishap. I knew if something like that had happened to me, it would have broken my concentration completely. For a second Perry seemed to lose his, and I grew sick with worry, afraid that after all his hard work, Perry would be undone by a dumb bird.

But I should have known better. In the following seconds Perry regained control and continued with his act as if nothing had gone amiss. Signaling offstage, he motioned for Lana to come back on with another, larger box mounted on low wheels. The box was held shut with a big gold padlock and had a black velvet drape placed on its top. After Perry spun the box around to show the audience its sides, Lana came back to center stage to open the padlock with an equally large gold key. From the opened box, she removed a black velvet sack and a gold rope, both of which she handed to Perry.

With broad gestures, Perry tied Lana's hands behind her back with the rope and then had her step inside the sack, which was now back in the box. Perry closed the sack over her head, helped her down into the box, and locked it securely.

The classical music stopped, and then there was an anticipatory roll of a solitary snare drum. Perry jumped on top of the box and held up the large black velvet drape which covered the box and his entire body. Amazingly, in the split second it took Perry to let the drape drop to the ground, he had disappeared, and Lana, let the drape drop to the ground, he had disappeared, and Lana, untied, was standing on the locked box!

This was hard enough to believe. But then Lana unlocked the padlock, opened the box, and pulled open the sack—and Perry emerged, now miraculously wearing a white tux!

The audience burst into applause. Modestly Perry bowed once, then quickly left the stage with Lana and his equipment while we were all still clapping. The wayward dove at last followed suit.

I turned to a relieved-looking Ingram family. "He was perfect. That last illusion was awesome!" I explained.

"That's my boy," Mr. Ingram said proudly.

"Metamorphosis has been one of my standards for years. But he made it look brand new."

As the applause died down, I followed the spotlight back to the master of ceremonies. "In a few minutes we will present our first award— for the Junior Magician of the Year."

Never have five minutes passed so *slowly*! The music started up again, and as we all waited for the decision, I couldn't help but add my own silent prayer on Perry's behalf. His finale had been so amazing I didn't think anyone would hold the disobedient dove against him. Then again, in a competition this intense, that kind of lapse might mean a lot. I hoped for his sake that Perry wasn't dwelling on that. In all other respects his routine had been perfect, his timing immaculate, a 9.9 on a scale of 10.

Finally the master of ceremonies returned to the stage. "I understand the judges have made their decision," he announced. "May I have the envelope, please?"

A cute little girl wearing an oversized top hat and an adorable pink tuxedo came out and handed the man a large white envelope. "And the winner is . . . Perry Ingram!"

The Ingrams and I hugged each other as Perry came back on stage to accept the gold trophy. He bowed deeply to the audience's thunderous applause and began to speak. "I'm not used to talking on stage. I usually express all my feelings through my performances. So forgive me if I don't have a fancy speech prepared. All I want to say is thank you. Thank you for making a dream come true."

Clutching the award close to his heart, Perry left the stage and started down the steps in front of the stage. Mr. Ingram got up and waved his hands to attract his son's attention. Smiling broadly, Perry approached the table and, still holding the trophy, gave his father a big bear hug. His mother, now unashamedly crying, rose to embrace him as well.

It wasn't until she let go of him that Perry even noticed me. In fantasizing about this moment, I'd visualized a shocked look on his face, a normal enough reaction to the sight of someone he didn't expect to see. But the shock would be replaced by a wide smile as his true feelings rose to the surface. He'd be happy I'd seen him at his finest, and in the rush of emotions he'd tell me so as he enveloped me in a loving embrace.

So I wasn't prepared for what really happened next. Perry saw me—I know he did—but said nothing and went over to shake his grandfather's hand.

I felt a tightening in my chest. Perry was ignoring me, and after all that had gone on, it was more than I could stand. I had to get as far away from this awful situation as possible. I threw my napkin down on the table, grabbed my purse, and ran. The ballroom was terribly long, but I finally reached the main exit and hurried out of it and through the lobby, finally taking refuge in a little mirrored alcove across from the ladies' lounge.

I gave in to my tears, but the relief I felt from releasing my pent-up emotions did nothing to soothe my hurt. I had figured Perry all wrong—just as his parents had. He didn't really care about me after all. He could relate to me when it came to working out card tricks, but that's as far as his interest went. His world consisted of magic, magic, and nothing but magic, and there was no room in it for me—or any other girl for that matter.

There was no use staying here any longer. I was too tired to cry any more, so I decided to find a pay phone and call my father. Retracing my steps, I turned out of the alcove, down the wide lobby adjacent to the ballroom—and there I confronted the puzzled eyes of Perry Ingram.

"Nicki, where are you going? Why are you leaving?"

"I've seen enough for one evening. I'm going home." I turned to move away from him, but he blocked my path.

"So soon? There are still more awards to be given out, and there'll be dancing later."

"I came to see you perform. Now I'm ready to leave."

Perry grasped my arm. "But you can't go now, Nicki. You said you came here to see me. Well, here I am."

· I shook loose from his hold. "I came to see you perform," I repeated. "My mistake, I realize now. Go on back to your parents, Perry. I won't bother you anymore." I began to walk away quickly but turned and, with all my heart, added, "By the way, congratulations on your award."

"Nicki, don't go!" Perry took off after me. "I'm glad you're here. Please don't leave me now."

Perry looked as if he might cry, and the sight was enough to set loose the tears that had been brimming in my eyes. "I don't understand you, Perry Ingram," I wailed in frustration. "I don't think I ever did. And now I'm tired of trying."

"I've really made a mess of things," Perry said, grabbing hold of my arm. "Listen, could we go somewhere and talk?"

It would have been foolish of me to leave then. Nodding silently, I followed Perry back to the alcove, which, if not private, at least afforded us a quiet place to talk. Perry loosened his bow tie as he sat down next to me. He looked very nervous but determined to speak.

"You don't know how much your being here means to me," he began.

"I see how much it means," I interrupted. "So much that you didn't even bother telling me you were up for an award. So much that you didn't bother calling me after you promised you would. So much that you treated me like a total stranger at your parents' table!"

"I'm trying to explain, Nicki," he said calmly. "I wasn't trying to avoid you. In fact, you don't know how many times I came close to calling you, to ask you to watch me practice, and to ask you to be here tonight."

"Well, why didn't you? Didn't you think I'd care?"

"It was because I knew you *would* care. I knew you liked me, Nicki, and what made it worse was that I liked you, too. I was scared about what might happen to my magic if I got more involved with you. And if things hadn't gone my way tonight, I would have hated to think you were to blame."

"I don't understand."

"Don't you see?" He threw his hands up. "Our timing was all wrong. If I were first meeting you now, everything would be different. But for the past few months, winning this award has been the most important thing in my life, and I wanted to devote all my energy and time to winning. I gave up track. I let my schoolwork slide. And I was ready to give up girls, too."

"And then you met me?"

"I liked you from the moment I met you at Sara's party. But when I realized you liked me, too, I panicked. I knew if I asked you out, we might get along really well. And then where would we have been? I knew I wouldn't have the time for dates, and I didn't want to wind up having to sacrifice my magic to be with you. So I walked out on you before anything had a chance to happen. I never expected to see you again, but when you showed up at the magic store the following week, I felt as if fate had stepped in and given me a second chance."

"Why didn't you tell me all of this back then?" I asked.

"I was going to—the night I invited you to the club. But when you left the club early, I figured I'd blown it with you. Then later when you asked me to be in your show, I was too caught up in my act to want to deal with a relationship. I figured as long as I knew I'd be seeing you for the show, I'd have at least one chance to get you interested in me again. In the meantime it was easier and safer for me to relate to you simply as a magician. That's why I didn't call you except to discuss magic. After that day at the club, I was afraid that if I even brought up the subject of dating, I'd lose my resolve and my concentration on my act. Can you understand that?"

"I do now, but if I'd known this before, it would have prevented an awful lot of aggravation and pain. I was going crazy wondering why you'd act like you liked me one minute but be indifferent the next. There's just one thing. I still don't understand why you ignored me at the table after you got your award."

"You ran off too soon, that's why," he said, finally showing me a smile. "Even though I didn't call you, I have been thinking about you a lot. So when I actually saw you tonight, I thought for a moment I was dreaming. It was unreal to me that you'd be here—as if I'd gone *poof* with my wand and made you appear. I turned away only for a few seconds, and then when I looked back you were gone. If Mom and Dad hadn't sworn to your having been there, I would have thought I was going nuts for sure."

"I guess I should have stayed. But I couldn't stand the thought that you didn't want me here. I'm glad I was wrong about that."

"By the way, how did you get here? Who invited you?"

"We don't have to get into that now," I answered. But Perry's eyes were insistent. I sighed. "Simon."

Perry furrowed his brows. "That figures," he said angrily. "And of course you accepted."

"I did it to see you," I explained.

But Perry didn't choose to hear that. "I was afraid he'd want you. We always did go after the same things," he said, more to himself than to me.

"Now wait a minute," I challenged. "You think he and I . . ." I shook my head.

"I don't know what to think. You asked him to be in your show, too. And he's got everything going for him that a girl could want."

"Like what? Don't forget who won Magician of the Year honors. You don't have to worry about Simon, Perry. He's got nothing on you."

"I wanted to win so badly. For me, of course. But for you, too. I wanted to impress you."

"You don't need a trophy for that. You're doing fine just being you."

"You really mean that?"

"Sure I do."

Tentatively I reached my hand out to stroke his. It was as if the touch alone were enough to break whatever invisible partitions we'd built between us. In a moment we were in each other's arms, holding one another as if we'd disintegrate into magic dust if we ever let go.

"Nicki, would you like to go out with me sometime soon?" Perry asked. He was still holding me tight, and I could feel the warmth of his breath caress my neck.

"I'd love to," I said. "But what about your magic?"

"That," he said, "can wait for the time being. Right now I can't think of anything I want more than this." And then he kissed me with the intensity of someone who'd had all his dreams come true.

Chapter Seventeen

I don't know how long we sat there. It must have been a long time, though, because by the time Perry's father found us, he looked flushed, as if he'd been running all over the hotel.

"So this is where you kids have been hiding? Perry, Mr. Kingsley has been looking all over for you. They're ready for you backstage."

"What for?"

"They want you to do an encore. Did you bring along any more props?"

"I always carry something extra up my sleeve, Dad." Perry winked and smiled.

"Go to it, boy. You don't have much time."

Perry got up quickly and straightened his tie. "Coming, Nicki?"

"I wouldn't miss watching you for anything."

"How'd you like to help me out?" he asked as we walked backstage.

"You mean assist you? What about Lana?"

"I think we'll let her sit this one out."

"Do you really mean it?" I shrieked. "But the trick. What do you want me to do?"

"It's simple. All you have to do is listen to what I tell you, and you'll be just fine."

"You're not going to try to stick any swords through me, are you?"

"No way." Perry put his arm around me and held me close as we walked inside.

Even though my part would be simple, I developed a mild case of stage fright as I waited to go on with Perry. In a matter of minutes I, Nicki Petersen, would be standing before the likes of Doug Henning, and I knew that the butterflies in my stomach would overwhelm me if I dwelled on that for too long. So I kept my focus on Perry, whose attention was concentrated on the details of his routine. Perry had heard that all of the winners might be called on to perform a final illusion, and he had brought along another prop just in case. It was a large trunk, and he was going to make me first appear in it and then disappear. As I scrunched down on a tiny ledge behind the trunk's false back panel, I looked up at Perry.

"What happens if you can't make me reappear?"

"Don't worry about that," he said reassuringly. "There's no way I'm going to let you disappear from my life now."

A few minutes later he wheeled me out to center stage. I couldn't be seen by the audience, though, so when Perry opened the trunk, it looked empty. Then he closed it and replaced the side and front panels with sheets of Plexiglas. The moment he started to slowly spin the trunk around, I was supposed to push my body against the false back so that I entered the main part of the trunk. By the time the glass front spun back toward the audience, I was snuggled inside, as if I'd been there all along. Perry then reversed the illusion, making me disappear again to the delight of the crowd. Needless to say, I was very happy when he made me reappear.

After the show I called my father to let him know he didn't have to pick me up after all. Perry drove me home in what he called his chariot, an old but serviceable Buick station wagon. But first he made a detour, exiting off the freeway toward a secluded spot on Mulholland Drive, where we gave each other our second kiss. The lights of the San Fernando Valley shimmered their approval back at us.

"I can't tell you how often I've imagined us right here under the stars," I told him. "How did you know I wanted to come here?"

"Oh, didn't I tell you? I've been practicing my mindreading skills." He kissed me gently on the nose. "Actually, this is something I've wanted to do for a long, long time."

I leaned back against the seat and sighed contentedly. My instincts had been right after all, I told myself, as I traced a finger along Perry's jawline. Sometimes fantasies can come true.

But just to reassure myself this was no dream, I pressed my lips to his and kissed him again and again and again.

Chapter Eighteen

Perry and I saw each other again the following afternoon, when he picked me up at my house for our first real date. Mom and Dad were pleased to discover that the boy I'd been driving all over the place to see turned out to be as sweet and decent as he was, and naturally Chris was thrilled to meet someone who could do magic tricks better than I could.

Then Perry in his white Adidas and I in my blue Nikes spent the next few hours at Balboa Park. Perry insisted we take advantage of the beautiful spring day by jogging through the lush green park, and I was so happy to be with him I didn't hesitate to agree. It was no surprise to me that Perry was in much better shape than I was, but somehow running didn't seem to be the arduous task it used to be. I said it was the company, but Perry theorized that after all this time, my muscles must have worked themselves into shape while I wasn't looking.

After our workout we set up a blanket between two cottonwood trees and watched an impromptu soccer match being played on a field in front of us.

Perry was the first to break the silence. "I got a call from Lana this morning," he said, twirling a blade of grass between his fingers. "She had a message she wanted me to give you."

I was lying on my stomach, but the mention of Lana's name was still enough to make me rise on my elbows. "What is it?" I asked anxiously.

Perry smiled. "She asked me to tell you that she regrets that she won't be able to make it to your magic show this Friday. In fact, she says that she's developed this sudden allergy to silver lamé, and she's not too sure she'll ever be able to assist me again. She was wondering if you'd like to take her place."

"Did you tell her I would?" I asked nervously.

"I'd never make a decision like that for you, Nicki. Especially not after all we've been through. But what do you say? Would you like to do it?"

"This being your assistant—it wouldn't mean I'd have to give up my card tricks, would it? Because I wouldn't want to do that."

"Of course not—though if there were such

a thing as an assistant card shuffler, I'd expect you to consider me for the position."

"I say yes, then."

"To letting me be your assistant card shuffler?"

"And to being your assistant, Mr. Ingram the Incomparable."

"Do you really mean it?"

"How's this for proof?" Pinning him to the blanket, I leaned over and gave him a kiss as sweet and satisfying as the ones we'd shared the night before.

That day only marked the beginning of a wonderful week. The following Tuesday, I walked into the reading center and was greeted by an excited Mary Beth, who was eager to read to me from a children's book on magic. Mrs. Radner had given her permission to use it as a substitute for the programmed reading, and Mary Beth did beautifully, sounding the words out clearly and showing perfect comprehension of the material. To prove the latter, after she'd finished reading, she insisted on doing one of the tricks described in the book. I told her about the House of Cards workshop for children. Who knows? She could be my first major discovery.

Perry was right about Lana wanting to retire from his act, and on the afternoon before my magic show, we met, and she told me all I needed to know to take over as Perry's assistant.

She turned out to be all right, too, even giving me some advice about Perry's likes and dislikes. ("Give him a bowl of chocolate ice cream, and he'll give you the world," she insisted.)

As for the show itself, well, it went off much better than I'd ever expected. Because it had become so big, though, I had to modify my card trick routine, turning it into a warm-up act for the elaborate illusions that followed. Instead of performing from the stage like the others, I walked through the audience, picking a different child to help me pull off each trick. Afterward, I became the mistress of ceremonies and introduced Simon, whose magic rings were a big hit with the kids. Then Perry enchanted the crowd with his doves. All this led up to the grand finale starring Mr. Ingram, who had practically every kid in the audience involved as an assistant in his act. He never once played down to the kids, and from my place behind the curtain, I spotted well over a hundred enchanted faces who'd be leaving the show spellbound by the wonders of magic. Mrs. Radner was delighted with the entire presentation and gave me a motherly hug right before we all took to the stage for our final curtain calls.

After the show ended, many teachers and parents came up from the audience and begged us to tell them how the illusions were done, but this was one time when we all kept close-mouthed. Some secrets are better left unexplained.

But as I was to find out, I had one last bit of magic to perform that afternoon. Sara and Caroline had come to watch the show, and, as I might have suspected, Sara was quite taken with Simon's smashing looks.

"Why have you been hiding him from me?" she demanded as soon as the show was over.

I didn't see any harm in introducing the two of them, so together we ran after Simon, catching up to him just as he was about to leave in his red Camaro Z-28. The results of the meeting surprised even me. Sara and Simon hit it off better than I'd even imagined, and the rest, as they say, is history. They've gone out twice so far, and from the way Sara croons the morning after each date, I have a feeling I'm going to be hearing a lot about the joys of Simon Kingsley for a long time to come.

The afternoon of the show, however, Perry was very surprised at my delight over the match. "How could you do that to your best friend?" he asked after I returned to the stage to tell him I'd made the introductions. "I thought you couldn't stand Simon."

"He's definitely not my type," I answered. "But if it hadn't been for his conceitedness, I'd never have gone to the awards dinner, and *we'd* probably never have gotten together. So I think that you and I both owe him a debt of gratitude."

"I never thought I'd be grateful to him for anything," Perry said. "It just goes to prove that you can never tell what a magician is going to do next." And there, right in the middle of the Santa Rosa Street School stage, Ingram the Invincible waved his magic wand over my head and made me disappear—right into his arms.

We hope you enjoyed reading this book. All the titles currently available in the Sweet Dreams series are listed on the next two pages. They are all available at your local bookshop or newsagent, though should you find any difficulty in obtaining the books you would like, you can order direct from the publisher, at the address below. Also, if you would like to know more about the series, or would simply like to tell us what you think of the series, write to:

Kim Prior,
Sweet Dreams,
Transworld Publishers Limited,
Century House,
61–63 Uxbridge Road,
London W5 5SA.

or
Kiri Martin
c/o Corgi & Bantam Books New Zealand,
9 Waipareira Avenue,
Henderson,
Auckland,
New Zealand.

To order books, please list the title(s) you would like, and send together with your name and address, and a cheque or postal order made payable to TRANSWORLD PUBLISHERS LIMITED. Please allow cost of book(s) plus 20p for the first book and 10p for each additional book for postage and packing.

Dear SWEET DREAMS reader,

*Since we started publishing SWEET DREAMS
almost two years ago, we have received
hundreds of letters telling us how much you like
the series and asking for details about
the books and the authors.*

*We are getting to know quite a lot about our
readers by now and we think that many of you
would like a club of your own. That's why we're
setting up THE SWEET DREAMS CLUB.*

*If you would like to become a member,
just fill in the details below and send it to me
together with a cheque or postal order
for £1.50 (payable to The Sweet Dreams Club)
to cover the cost of our postage and administration.
Your membership package will contain a special
SWEET DREAMS membership card,
and a SWEET DREAMER newsletter packed
full of information about the books and authors,
beauty tips, a fascinating quiz and lots more
besides (including a fabulous special offer!).*

Now fill in the coupon (in block capitals please), and send, with
payment, to:

The Sweet Dreams Club,
Freepost (PAM 2876),
London W5 5BR.

N.B. No stamp required.

I would like to join The Sweet Dreams Club.

Name:..

Address:..

....

I enclose a cheque/postal order for £1.50, made payable to The Sweet
Dreams Club.